# An Annoyance of Grackles

Applied Topology Book 3

Margaret Ball

Galway Publishing

Copyright 2018 Margaret Ball
Published by Galway Publishing

ISBN Paperback: 978-1-947648-10-4
ISBN eBook: 978-1-947648-11-1

Printed in the United States of America
Cover art: Cedar Sanderson
Formatting: Polgarus Studio

# 1. Sometimes a grackle is just a grackle

He was shouting my name.

"Thalia! Thalia, *don't*!"

"Lensky?"

The room was dim; it must be very early morning. I could just see that his eyes were closed. His whole body jerked spasmodically as he drew breath for another shout.

I shook his shoulder. "Lensky, wake up, you're having a bad dream!"

That didn't wake him, so I went to emergency measures: an elbow in the ribs.

"Thalia! Ow! Don't…"

His eyes opened. He breathed heavily for a few moments. "Ah, was I snoring?"

"Dreaming. I think. You were shouting at me not to do something."

A relieved huff. "Well, what's new about that?"

And after a moment, "You're sure I wasn't shouting at you to quit elbowing me like that?"

"That was after."

"Oh, well. Sorry to wake you." He rolled over on his side and closed his eyes.

I deployed my elbow again. "Tell me."

"Mmm? Never can remember dreams."

"You've been having this one for a week. I want to know what's going on with you."

With a sigh, Lensky rolled onto his back and clasped his hands behind his head. "Do we have to do this at oh-dark-thirty?"

"Yes, because you've been dodging my questions all week and this time I'm not waiting until you get your defenses back in place."

He sighed again. "All right. I've been having this dream."

I waited.

"You're about to teleport someplace, and somehow I know you shouldn't, it's a trap. I shout at you to stop but you just - disappear. And I know I'll never see you again."

"I was afraid it was something like that." I'd almost been expecting it. That didn't make me any happier. "You've done your best to accept my paranormal abilities. But obviously there's a level where you can't accept them, where you equate my using my abilities with your losing me." In the long run, no outsider could accept them. I should have known better than to think Lensky would be different. He'd held out longer than Rick the Rat, but now even he couldn't take it any more.

"Oh, stop with the pop psychology! I *do* accept your abilities. It's not about that. It's about Blondie, if you must know."

"You dream about a terrorist bomber? That's kinky."

"Bomber, yes, but maybe not a terrorist. The analysts at the Agency have been doing some digging; they've learned a lot from the papers you got out of his safe last fall. I'm not supposed to tell you much about it, but I can say this much: he may have identified me in October, and through me he may have identified you. If he goes after you… He won't. If it even looks like he's getting close, I'll see to it that you're safe. But just for a few days, would you humor me? Ride in to the office with me?"

"All right."

"*Promise*? You won't get impatient and teleport yourself?"

"Yes. I promise. Now go back to sleep."

"Not much chance of that now," he grumbled. Instead he got up and started coffee, and we watched the January sunrise stain the cloudy sky red. His condo had been built by somebody who understood Austin. Big windows to the west are virtually useless; you have to keep them covered for nine months of the year or you'll cook in the afternoon sun. Big windows to the east are much, much better. In the case of Lensky's condo, they gave us a view of a narrow strip of trees following a seasonal creek, and above the trees, a broad sweep of sky.

About the time I finished my first cup of coffee, a swarm of grackles rose from the trees. They took flight like a cloud of shadows, whirling and screeching and re-forming in mid-air before settling among the trees again. I shivered.

Lensky could worry about the terrorist bomber, but "Blondie" was only human, with only human abilities. I was much more worried about the Master of Ravens.

***

Parking on the UT campus is never fun, but Lensky has a really good permit and today we got there early enough to park quite close to Allandale House, the Victorian mansion whose third floor housed the Center for Applied Topology. All the same, getting from the parking space to the office required us to walk under live oaks where more grackles perched. It crossed my mind that it was just about impossible for anyone to enter and leave Allandale House by conventional means without being observed by an annoyance of grackles. (Yes, that really is the collective noun; I looked it up.) Seemed to me that teleporting was not only more convenient but safer; pop out of the condo and into the private side of the Center, with no grackles involved.

Still, I wasn't the one having nightmares.

And I had no reason to believe that the Master of Ravens was even in Austin, let alone plotting another attack on the Center. It's just that I felt about idle grackles much as our director, Dr. Verrick, feels about topologists at loose ends: trouble waiting to happen.

Sometimes, I told myself, a grackle is just a grackle. And that's quite bad enough.

The office was empty when Lensky and I got there, but it didn't stay that way for long. By the time I had settled Mr. M. at my desk there were promising noises from the public side. Annelise, our receptionist and resident fabulist, had come in with a box of fresh doughnuts. Ben Sutherland had come with her, naturally. "Do you commute with Annelise just to make sure you get first crack at the doughnuts?" I asked him. It wasn't a totally unreasonable question. Our most innovative research fellow when it comes to finding new paranormal applications for topology, he has an innovative approach to eating as well, involving things like chocolate with root beer or pizza with anchovies and pineapple as well as a serious doughnut addiction. I figure he stays slim because all that stuff isn't really food. At least Annelise had broken him of the habit of buying shirts that were way too large because he couldn't be bothered to try anything on. Or maybe she was just buying his shirts for him now.

"We'll need them this morning," he said without actually answering the question. "Staff meeting at ten."

"Break room?"

"That or your office. It's research fellows only."

"Break room." My office was actually big enough to accommodate all four research fellows and Dr. Verrick, but I didn't want them making a habit of it.

I'd thought that Ben and I would have a leisurely morning of sipping coffee, picking out the best doughnuts, and swapping notes on our research. But Colton Edwards came through from the private side only ten minutes later, and Ingrid Thorn actually came up the stairs like a normal person.

"I think they've got the break room bugged," Ben groused. "Have you noticed how everybody shows up at once when Annelise sets out new doughnuts? And *he* doesn't even need one," he said, mock-scowling at Lensky.

"They also serve who only spook and spy," Lensky said equably. "And you don't need them nearly as much as you used to." He took a cruller back to his office; he didn't enjoy meetings any more than the rest of us, and according to Ben he wasn't expected to attend this one.

What Lensky said was true – about the doughnuts, I mean. We'd started having these periods of feeling very shaky about the time our research really began to pay off, late last spring. The twinkling lights we called "stars," brought by Mr. M. from ancient Babylon, functioned as amplifiers for the effects we achieved by applied topology alone. A logical consequence was that when we started teleporting across town instead of teleporting two feet across the office floor, we needed to eat more – a lot more. It wasn't all that surprising; topologists have always been fueled by coffee and doughnuts. It's just that the doughnut part got a whole lot more important after our research took off.

Different kinds of work exert different drains on our bodies. Camouflage, which is really just a kind of bending the light, is not that demanding. With telekinesis, it depends on the weight of the object you're moving and the distance you want it to go. (There is some kind of relationship between what we do and classical physics; we're just not exactly sure what it is.)

Teleportation, which by definition implies moving your own weight and often requires you to move somebody else's weight as well, had been our worst energy-sucker up to now, and even that was getting better. Last spring, teleporting across town required serious refueling. By fall we could jump halfway across the state – and Texas is not exactly a small state. This winter the chief limiting factor on our range was identifying places to teleport to, because with some exceptions we have to visualize the destination very clearly before jumping. Our adviser – that would be Mr. M., not Dr. Verrick - said we were building mental muscles as we practiced.

"I'm going to need muscles *and* doughnuts when I start flying," Colton said, enveloping a sour cream twist in one of his big hands. If he ever found a topological analog to flight, we'd probably have to triple our doughnut fund; it was going to take a lot of fuel to lift that body. He wasn't fat, just large. All over. And he made it worse by wearing big, clunky boots that were a hazard to innocent bypassers.

Ben and I rolled our eyes. Flight had been Colton's obsession since he was hired on last fall. His single-minded concentration on the problem had resulted in a lot of six-inch falls, three annoyed topologists, and – as a grand finale – a three-story fall from *above* his office to the ground just outside the building. In that last episode he'd managed to hook one of his boots over a balcony railing and suffered a severe sprain that left him on crutches for days. After the experience of nearly killing himself, followed by the experience of being surrounded by angry topologists telling him not to even *think* about pulling that again, he'd kept his flying experiments reasonably quiet. But we all knew he was still working on it.

"You haven't given up yet?"

"Um. I think I've been following the wrong angle, trying to expand teleportation. Ingrid suggested we look at path-connected spaces." He nodded as Ingrid came into the room, slightly out of breath, and offered her a sour cream glazed doughnut. As usual, she looked as if she'd just stepped out of a time machine and hadn't caught on to modern fashions yet. She wore her silver-blond hair in braids wrapped around her head, and she seemed to have an inexhaustible supply of white blouses which she wore buttoned up to the collar. I do understand about vintage clothes – I spend a lot of time at Buffalo Exchange looking for classic rock T-shirts – but Ingrid's blouses always looked brand new. And she *ironed* them. I know this because, technically, I share an apartment with her, though I don't use it much since Lensky bought his condo.

The really annoying thing was that even dressed like somebody's maiden aunt, she was a knockout. There'd been fender-benders on the Drag caused by students appreciating her figure, and the coronet of braids framed an icy but perfect face.

"Thanks, but I don't need a doughnut," Ingrid said. "I drove in today."

She'd been doing that a lot in the last couple of months. I wondered if she too had been having nightmares.

She glanced around the room. "Isn't Mr. M. coming?"

"Technically, he's not a research fellow. And he gets drowsy in the cold weather. He's taking another nap."

She smiled faintly. "Probably just as well. If you gave him any coffee he might start singing in the middle of the meeting."

Dr. Verrick stumped to the head of the table and regarded the four of us with the expression of a man who's requested a SEAL team and received four of the Seven Dwarfs. At an age somewhere between seventy and a hundred and ten (none of us had the nerve to ask), you'd think he would have got used to people not living up to his expectations.

"In a few minutes," Dr. Verrick announced, "you will have the opportunity to meet a young man who will be interning with the research department this semester. He will, of course, receive significantly less than a full research fellow's stipend."

That was an eyebrow-raiser. Considering the beggarly stipends he allotted full-fledged research fellows, the only way an intern could receive significantly less was if he paid for the privilege of working with us. And nobody was that crazy, unless…

"Oh, God," I said involuntarily, "Tell me it's not Vern Trexler."

"Staff selection is entirely *my* prerogative," Dr. Verrick said, and paused long enough for me to have one of those near-death experiences where your whole life zips past your eyes. I hadn't had nearly enough life for this to take more than a couple of seconds; I was kind of counting on another fifty or sixty years of experiences to stockpile before getting to this bit.

"But no, Miss Kostis, the person I have in mind is not Mr. Trexler, but rather an exceptionally talented dissertation candidate who requires a brief sabbatical from his formal work." I swear he enjoyed watching me start to melt down. Trexler – well, that's another story. *Not*, praise gods and little stars, part of this one.

Nobody had ever suggested the Center for Applied Topology as a rest cure for troubled minds. We were more likely to shatter minds than heal them. Ben made that point and Dr. Verrick said testily,

"Exactly what gave you the impression that Mr. Bhatia was seeking a rest cure? I expect he will work harder here than he has in the entire rest of his academic career, and it will do him good."

"Prakash Bhatia? *That* Bhatia?" Ingrid exclaimed. Maybe she knew the guy from graduate school. I'd have to get any juicy details out of her as soon as the meeting was over.

"Yes, *that* Bhatia," Dr. Verrick confirmed. He went on to tell us that at this late stage in his studies, Prakash Bhatia had begun experiencing the minor, disturbing incidents that had drawn all of us – the research fellows, anyway – to the Center. Unlike us, though, he was determined to deny that anything unusual was going on. He *hadn't* collected all the spades in play during a bridge game and spread them out in order on the table, somebody was playing conjuring games. He *didn't* correct a research paper without touching it, he'd just forgotten that he had already edited it on the computer. And so forth and so on.

Continuous denial of reality is not good for the mind. Dr. Verrick hoped that being in contact with four research fellows who routinely did things a lot more amazing than messing with hands of cards would help Prakash Bhatia to accept the reality of his talent. But taking him in for this semester was not a work of charity; this young man had a lot to contribute to our work, if he could just let go of his crippling certainties.

He dismissed us back to our offices, saying that we should be prepared to interview the new intern in a few minutes. And that refusing to accept the appointment was *not* an option. We were going to work with Bhatia for a semester. Instead of giving him a conventional interview, he expected us to explain the structure and work of the Center for Applied Technology.

# 2. We try not to disturb normal people

Once we were back on the private side, I accepted my own bit of reality. If this wasn't really an interview, then we might as well talk to this Bhatia as a group; maybe that would make him less likely to dismiss any one research fellow's claims. And my office was the only one large enough for all four of us to sit in. I suggested to Ben and Colton that they drag in some extra chairs.

This was going to be an extra chore for afterwards, putting those chairs back where they came from. As I may have mentioned, my strategy for discouraging visitors was not having anything around for them to sit on.

I should probably explain about the private side. You may have gathered that we try not to disturb normal people by accidentally giving them glimpses of our research results.

Ben and I, in our fourth year of studying with Dr. Verrick, had been the first to discover that we could make strange little things happen in the real world by visualizing some topological theorems or constructs and mentally linking them with real objects or places. Fortunately for us, Dr. Verrick was every bit as loyal to the undergraduates in his Topology Honors Program as to the graduate students whom he guided through comprehensives, qualifiers, and dissertation. He believed us! Not only that; he wrote letters and pulled strings and created a place for us: the Center for Applied Topology, funded by a semi-anonymous intelligence agency, housed by the University of Texas. UT generously gave us a space nobody else wanted: the third floor of Allandale House, a Victorian mansion incongruously sitting among UT's buildings and protected by the terms of Chester Allandale's will.

One of the first things we did with the third floor was to partition it. Someone coming up the stairs now would see an oddly proportioned room with a wall just to the right of the stairs. But they wouldn't check to see what was behind that wall, because there was no door in it. (There had been one, briefly, last fall, but we took care of *that* little problem as soon as we got rid of the idiot who had it put in.)

The only way to get into the private side was to visualize a Möbius strip at right angles to the wall, and then to walk that imaginary strip until it deposited you on the other side. Or, if you weren't a topologist, to get one of us to take you by the arm and walk you across. That didn't happen often, because the crossing tended to make non-topologists seasick.

On this side of the wall there were offices for Dr. Verrick and for the four research fellows – that would be Colton, Ingrid, Ben and me – and several empty offices testifying to Dr. Verrick's optimism about recruiting more topologists. On the public side were a rather large general area, the break room – otherwise known as the beating heart of the Center, with a coffee maker and occasional doughnuts - a desk for our receptionist Annelise, and offices for the other support staff: Jimmy DiGrazio for computer hackery, Meadow Melendez for robotics, Bradislav Lensky for liaison with the funding agency.

"I'm beginning to dislike this guy already," Ben grumbled. "I want to keep exploring Riemann surfaces, not try to explain the Center to someone who's already decided not to believe in it."

"If you're messing with Riemann surfaces again," said Ingrid, "maybe you'd better get a fireplace put in." Ben's first attempts to generate light via Riemann surfaces had instead generated enough fire to set off the alarms and start the automatic sprinkler system.

"Maybe," I said hopefully, "he won't be able to cross the wall. Dr. Verrick did imply he was leaving Bhatia to figure that out on his own, didn't he?"

"You can't trust what Dr. Verrick implies," Ingrid said.

"Well, anyway… if he *does* cross the wall, maybe the experience will open his mind a tiny bit."

Ingrid gave me a sour look. "What have you been doing, Thalia, reading one of those pop psychology articles on Leadership?"

Actually, it had been a pop psychology article on Optimism, claiming that optimistic people were happier and had better relationships than pessimists. I'd thought it was worth trying out, but the attitude change was somewhat more challenging than I'd realized.

Footsteps just outside, in the hall! Definitely on *this* side of the wall. So he'd passed the first test.

The man who entered was tall, dark haired, somewhat dark skinned – think coffee with a generous dollop of cream – and looked to be pissed off already. He was super-formally dressed for a college campus: white button-down shirt, dark red tie, tailored dark gray pants and a matching vest, and I bet there was a suit coat somewhere to complete the outfit.

Oh, and one more thing. He was devastatingly handsome. Movie-star-level good looks. We were to learn that he was all too aware of this fact, but in this moment of relative ignorance I just happily enjoyed the eye candy. In some ways, Intern Bhatia would constitute quite an upgrade to this office.

"The Center for Applied Topology?"

"Research Division," I said. "Congratulations on passing the wall."

He ignored me and talked over my head to Ben. "I have been hearing many things about this so-called Center. Most recently have I been hearing that you have persuaded Miss Thorn to drop out of graduate school in favor of this… research." He said the last word with all the enthusiasm of somebody identifying dog poop.

"If you know Miss Thorn at all," Ben said with a tight smile, "you must know how very unlikely it is that I – or anyone else – could persuade her to a course of action contrary to her own judgment."

"I would have been thinking this also," said Bhatia, "but she is only a woman. She may have been led astray, or perhaps this is way to conceal that her mind is not strong enough for the rigors of doctoral program."

Ingrid jumped to her feet. "If you want to insult me to my face, Bhatia, at least *look* at me while you're doing it!"

"There, there," he said, making little patting motions in her direction. "You see, feminine emotionalism. Not so good for pure mathematics, isn't it?" He looked back at Ben. "I am only wishing to make it clear that your Center will not affect *me* in the same way. Because Doctor Verrick is my dissertation adviser I take his advice to come here for one semester only, then I shall return to real mathematics department."

"I think we can bear up under the loss," Ben said tightly. "Look, Mr. Bhatia…"

"Not Batia, Bhatia."

"Batia."

"No, Bhatia. Bha, ta, ya."

"Bataya."

"Not Ba, *Bha*. And not ta ya, *tya*."

(Sigh) "Ok, how about we just call you Prakash?"

"Since you are unable to pronounce my last name correctly, that is perhaps least painful option."

"Okay," Ben said through gritted teeth, "Prakash it is. I just wouldn't want you to leap to the conclusion that I'm being friendly or anything by using your first name."

Prakash indicated that, being such an easy-going fellow himself, he could sympathize with Ben's feeling awkward at addressing a Tata Institute M.A. by his first name.

It didn't get any better after that. He looked down his nose at Ben and Colton because they had only bachelor's degrees, he found half a dozen ways to imply that Ingrid had lost the respect of the entire mathematics department when she gave up "real" research for "*this*," and he was apparently incapable of seeing or hearing me at all. Well, you know… another peon with no advanced degrees, and female, and *short*…. I guess it was just too, too painful for him to contemplate the prospect of a semester spent around such a nobody.

Optimism is probably overrated, anyway.

When we finally got rid of him, we tried to toss around some ideas for Colton's flight project. It wasn't a good day for it: all four of us were spitting grit after a morning with the Blessed Prakash. Ingrid and Colton didn't have the patience to explain how they expected path-connected spaces to let them defy gravity, and Ben and I didn't have the patience to follow any explanations we couldn't understand immediately.

Eventually Colton, at least, had a worthwhile breakthrough. He looked out the window and said, "It's getting late. And all we're doing is bickering. I think we should reconvene in a better location."

"And you had in mind?"

"Hole in the Wall is just across the Drag. And their happy hour has already started."

That proposition passed with unanimous consent and no bickering.

I stopped on our way out to leave Mr. M. with Lensky. Now that he had taken up singing as a hobby, I was kind of afraid to take him any place where there might be live music.

"You're going to some place where there might be live music?" He seemed less than thrilled to hear of my plans. "Do you want me to wait and drive you back?"

"I don't know how long we'll be," I said. "After meeting the Blessed Prakash, the entire research division is on the verge of insurrection. Sorry we didn't invite you, but this is kind of a topologists-only bitch session. Look, you go on home and I'll teleport back to your place when we break up. There can't be a safer place to teleport into than a spy's condo."

"I have no desire to be ground zero at your critical mass," Lensky said. "Go, go. Come over afterwards and I'll let you chop the garlic."

"What a tempting offer!"

"Those who chop no garlic, get no *Capelli Livornese*." Lensky had recently displayed a surprising talent for cooking, mostly Italian. I had no clue what Capelli Livornese was, but based on past performance it would be something I wouldn't want to miss.

The sky was covered with light gray clouds when we came out of Allandale House. The intertwined black branches of the winter trees exploded into a mass of moving black shapes that rose and wheeled, dancing against the bright clouds, and settled again. I zipped up my jacket. It wasn't that cold, but I was that chilled.

# 3. The Mathematical Mafia

Even with Happy Hour prices, Hole in the Wall wasn't quite as good a deal as Scholz's; they sold their beer by the bottle, not by the pitcher. On the other hand, ever since I'd carelessly given myself a hangover with too many pitchers of Scholz's beer on my first date with Lensky, I'd been promising myself that I'd cut back to drinking by the glass, not the pitcher.

I did not inhale my first Lone Star. I just stared at the bottle.

"Are you going to drink that or just flirt with it?" Ben asked. He'd chugged his first bottle and was already signaling for another.

"I'm getting too old for serious drinking during the week. I'm cutting back."

Ben brushed his hair out of his eyes. I thought of suggesting to Annelise that she make regular haircuts her next project, now that she finally had him wearing clothes that were designed for his tall, narrow body type. "With respect, Lia, this is one hell of a time to go on the wagon."

"I said cutting back, not giving it up. I'm going to take the time to taste and savor every sip."

"Maybe you'd better switch to Scotch, then. I don't think you can sip beer fast enough to neutralize the Prakash Effect."

"I don't think there *is* enough beer for that." I tilted the bottle and rolled a mouthful of Lone Star around on my tongue.

"He's not all bad," Ingrid said. Coming from her, that was practically a glowing recommendation. Then again, coming from her, it might just be a statement about his mathematical ability.

"Oh, right. You know him. Give!"

"It's more that I know who he is, that's all."

"You didn't have any classes together?" Disappointing, that. I'd been hoping she had some secret data on Bhatia that we could use to beat him into shape.

"No, he didn't do any of his course work here, he's an import. The Tata Institute asked Dr. Verrick to oversee his dissertation because they don't have anyone in general topology who's up on Prakash's chosen topic."

That was an unusual thing for a rival university to admit, but we'd heard it before. Dr. Verrick's Honors Topology course and the follow-on graduate program had produced so many successful mathematicians that even Ivy League schools had been known to try and insert their students for a couple of semesters, and there was no shortage of graduate students trying to transfer into the department. If Bhatia had gotten to the head of that line, he must be really sharp.

"How long has he been here?"

"Started in June."

Last June, we'd been extremely busy recovering from the havoc wreaked by the Master of Ravens. Last June, Lensky had come back from DC with the news that his agency was assigning him to work with us permanently because they'd decided we were a valuable resource and "you maniacs need somebody sane to watch out for you." Last June, I probably wouldn't have noticed a Tyrannosaurus Rex being admitted to the Ph.D. program, as long as it was a polite Tyrannosaurus, didn't step on our offices and ate only education majors.

"Well, *I* noticed him," Ingrid said. "Okay, he's a jerk, but you've got to admit he's great eye candy. He joined a cricket team about ten minutes after he registered, and they played all summer. Wait until you see him in his cricket whites, Lia!" She fanned herself.

And he could make Ingrid respond like an actual human female. That could become *interesting.* And it wasn't going to make Jimmy DiGrazio, our resident computer nerd and Ingrid's boyfriend, happy. About the only thing Jimmy had going for him in the way of looks was that he was taller than Ingrid.

"We're only stuck with him for one semester," Colton reminded her. He pushed floppy yellow hair away from his forehead. Unlike Ben, he got it cut that way on purpose. And on him it looked good.

"I may have to kill him before it gets warm enough for cricket again." Lone Star wasn't really designed for serious savoring; I killed that bottle and ordered a local artisanal beer that was only affordable during happy hour.

"He's a pill," Colton conceded, "but he *did* walk through the wall, and that without any of us telling him to use a Möbius strip. If he can call up the relevant math without even thinking about it, that's some serious talent there."

"Which he absolutely denies having."

"Well, yes. I can see why Dr. Verrick considers him a hard nut to crack. But when he accepts the reality of what he can do, he could be a fantastic member of our team." Colton was still working on his first beer. I need a minimum of three drinks to achieve that level of cockeyed optimism. But then, Colton is a genuinely nice person, and nobody ever accused me of that.

"I don't know," said Ben gloomily. "I'm afraid that when this nut cracks, he'll go nuts."

"Good!" Well, I *told* you I'm not a nice person.

"Can I help crack him?" Neither is Ingrid.

Colton frowned at all three of us.

"It's not very kind, talking that way. And Ingrid, I thought you at least liked him to look at."

Ingrid gave him one of her patented Norse-goddess freezing looks. "*Prakash* may think that women are weak and emotional, but that's his problem. I am entirely capable of appreciating his perfectly chiseled lips while finding him too insufferably conceited to live."

"Better not discuss his perfectly chiseled lips with Jimmy, though," I said, just to bring her back into touch with reality.

Despite what I'd told Lensky, we did not spend much more time griping about Prakash. The subject was too depressing. As I sipped my second beer we rambled through such gripping topics as the chances for seeing actual snow in Austin this winter, the practical uses of N-manifolds, the apartment Ben and Annelise had just rented, whether Lindelöf spaces would be better for personal shields, loose ends remaining for the Center after an extremely fraught fall semester, and the skiing and snowboarding competitions in Sweden. I had nothing to contribute to the last bit. I've always thought of skiing as a sign of insanity: surely the top of a snow-covered mountain is the *last* place where you'd want to put yourself in a position of unstable equilibrium? And I wasn't clear on what snowboarding even was. Like waterboarding? Only colder?

"Going home," I announced when the second beer was done.

"Wait a minute," Ben said. "Annelise wants to have a party to celebrate us getting this apartment."

"Well, that's your problem."

Ben gulped. "I already said yes. As long as it's just Center people. Saturday night."

That was short notice. Annelise probably didn't want to wait long enough for Ben to get cold feet. As long as it really was just the Center for Applied Topology staff, it should be okay. Strangers would be a different story. Most topologists don't socialize well; new people are stressful, and Prakash had been quite enough stress for one week.

I worked my way to the bathroom at the back of the bar, made sure the door was closed but not locked, and teleported.

The condo smelled wonderful. I followed the scent to the kitchen, where Lensky handed me a chef's knife and a head of garlic.

Chopping and sautéing and simmering, all the support tasks of cooking that I'd had no patience for when Mom tried to teach me so that I could catch a man, took on another flavor entirely when I was doing them in the company of the man who'd caught me. But then, with Lensky, the sous-chef jobs didn't come with lectures about my personal life. It was just, "Can you cut these into this size chunks?" or, "Sauté this in a little olive oil until the onions are translucent."

Turns out, I liked cooking just fine; it was the sauce of "you're-a-disappointment-to-us" I found so bitter.

It may have helped that I wasn't required to do any planning. Chop this, stir that, peel these, the string of minor tasks ran on without hurry or drama or people screaming at each other in the middle of the kitchen, and things just kept smelling better and better until it was time to bake the pasta dish or slow-simmer the sauce or whatever, and then we'd share glasses of whatever wine Lensky was putting in the sauce that day and I'd lean back against him and he'd put his arms around me.

And the food was pretty good, too.

On this particular evening I wielded the chef's knife so ferociously that I reduced half a head of garlic to a mound of garlic paste before Lensky gently reclaimed the knife. "The new guy must be a disaster if you've still got so much nervous energy after blowing off steam with the rest of the Mathematical Mafia for two hours. What did you do, talk so much that you forgot to drink your beer?"

I started to wipe the sweat out of my eyes, remembered the garlic on my hands at the last minute and settled for drawing the back of one wrist across my forehead. "There is not enough beer in the world to reconcile me to working with Prakash Bhatia," I told him, "so I decided to spare myself the hangover that would result from trying."

"It took you guys two hours to trash the man? You can't know that much about him yet."

"Don't underestimate him," I said. "Every time he opened his mouth he offended at least two of us, frequently in three different directions. Anyway, that wasn't all we talked about."

"What else?"

"Oh, all kind of things. Ben and Annelise's new place – oh, they're having an apartment-warming party Saturday. Grackles... Loose ends... Whether we're going to have to defend the Center against the Master of Ravens again." Calling himself first Raven Crowson and then Jay Corbin, this wizard with power drawn from black birds had first threatened Lensky's niece and me in a bid to halt an investigation into his business, and afterwards had tried to destroy the entire Center in revenge for our disruption of his profitable sex trafficking operation. We had no idea where he'd disappeared to after the failure of that last attack.

There was a very good reason why those clouds of grackles wheeling over Allandale House had made me nervous.

Lensky dropped the garlic paste into the deep iron skillet, stirred for a moment, and poured white wine over it. After adding sliced onions, chopped parsley and diced tomatoes he pushed the skillet to the back of the stove and filled two stemless wine glasses with generous splashes of the white wine. I inhaled appreciatively.

"You'd done most of the work before I got here. Sorry about that."

"Just as well, this time. After seeing what you did to a head of garlic I'd be afraid to turn you loose on an innocent bunch of parsley."

"Unfortunately, a chef's knife isn't much use against an annoyance of grackles."

Lensky gave the simmering sauce another stir, pulled out a kitchen chair for himself, and drew me down to sit on his lap. "I'd bet on the Mathematical Mafia against the Master of Ravens any day," he said, "and don't forget, you've got me for backup. And more, if you need; I can call in some old favors back at the home office." He set his wine glass on the table, then took mine and set it beside his. He liked to secure all spillable items before starting anything.

With dinner simmering and the wine out of the way, he wrapped his arms around me and nuzzled the back of my neck. "If I run into anybody calling himself Maître Corbeau or Señor Cuervo I'll be sure to let you know." He nibbled very delicately along the edge of an earlobe and I shivered.

Then his lips moved on down to the side of my neck, and the last practical thing I said for some time was, "Should we turn down the heat under that skillet?"

"Might as well," he murmured into my neck, "I don't want to put in the shrimp until five minutes before we eat."

"Oh, is this going to take more than five minutes?"

Over a very late dinner – we hadn't thrown in the shrimp or started the pasta until the last minute - he said thoughtfully, "Speaking of loose ends, I've got permission to tell you why I'm so worried about Blondie. I still can't tell you everything, but at least I can go over my personal history with him."

"Blondie," real name unknown, was a demolitions specialist who'd come to the attention of the intelligence community after a series of terrorist bombings of large buildings that all had the same "signature." Lensky's three-letter agency had discovered last fall that Blondie had entered the US illegally across the southern border. They'd tracked him as far as a luxury Riverwalk hotel in San Antonio and then Lensky had enlisted my help in finding out which of the three possible targets was the real "Blondie." The op had been semi-successful. The 'successful' part was that an unauthorized peek in the targets' room safes had made it easy to identify him, and as long as we were snooping Lensky had taken snapshots of the papers in Blondie's safe which he sent back to the home office for translation and analysis.

The 'semi' part was that I had needed to be physically close to Blondie's room safe to transfer the papers back into it, and while we were standing outside his suite he'd opened his door and gotten a glimpse of Lensky and me before I teleported us out of there.

Lensky's bosses had felt that the information gleaned from Blondie's papers was useful enough to balance the fact that he'd been alerted to the surveillance, so we hadn't taken too much grief from above about the unplanned ending of the op. And we hadn't seen or heard from Blondie again, discounting one very odd night when he'd been spotted mingling with the guests at a high-dollar shindig right here in Austin, so he had rather faded from my mind.

"For one thing, there's been some chatter linking him to this area."

"From last October?" That had been the time of the peculiar party incident.

"No. Just this week, actually. The other thing is, some of what our analysts turned up may explain how he happened to show up at that party. They think he's a Romanian national."

"So?" That did surprise me a little, given the number of notes in Arabic that we'd extracted from his safe. But not that much, given that he was tall and very blond.

"Remember my saying he looked vaguely familiar? After the San Antonio incident?"

"No… but we were both somewhat, um, distracted after I teleported us out of there to your condo."

"I remember. You passed out and scared the dickens out of me. Hell of a time to do that, too."

"That was a *long* jump. I didn't realize how much I'd need to refuel. Anyway, I made it up to you later, didn't I?"

He smiled. "*Oh*, yes. I *love* being with you when you've just come skidding and slithering out of the 'in-between.'"

"And I love being with you when you've just been shot at and missed," I said to remind him that I hadn't been the only enthusiastic participant in that little episode.

Lensky cleared his throat. "Yes. Well. I was stationed in Romania for a couple of years."

"You never mentioned that."

"It was some time ago… Because they believe in making maximum use of our existing skills, and because I'm fluent in Polish, the agency naturally wanted to send me to Eastern Europe. But because it's still a *government* agency, they put me in Bucharest rather than Warsaw."

"Oh well, at least you already knew one Slavic language."

"Romanian is a *Latin* language. I'd have been more effective practically anywhere else in Eastern Europe. Anyway, while I was there we had a massive security breach. Not my doing; an idiot at the Embassy failed to follow protocols. But I was burned and so were two other people. They whisked us out of there and into other posts immediately. But you see, I think I did encounter Blondie there, if only briefly. And he'd have known who I was and where I worked. When he saw us in San Antonio, he might have remembered that connection. It wouldn't have taken much digging among his contacts to find out that I was currently stationed in Austin, with the Center for Applied Topology. That much could have led him to the Moore Foundation party. Where he would have seen you again. With me again. And now one of my agents may have spotted him here in Austin just this week. It may be nothing, but - keep your eyes open?"

"Sure," I promised, and then thought I had a chance to make a point.

"Now aren't you glad you asked me to help in San Antonio?"

"Why?"

"If I hadn't been with you then, I wouldn't know what he looks like and I wouldn't be able to help you watch for him."

"If I hadn't taken you with me," Lensky said gloomily, "*he* wouldn't know what *you* look like and I would be much happier about this entire situation."

Well, that was another way to look at it.

# 4. The Boogie-Woogie Bugle Turtle

*"You want to talk to me."*

*"I don't recall issuing an invitation."*

*"I heard."*

*"From whom?"*

*"Around. That's not the important question. The question is, 'How much?'"*

*"How... mercenary."*

*"Yes, that's what I am. Tell me the size of the job and I'll tell you what my fee will be."*

*The tall, lithe man dressed in black nearly faded into the shadows of his host's room, save for his short blond, almost white hair. The other man, short and dark with a five o'clock shadow, was physically less impressive, but was attended by a crackling sense of power that would have intimidated anyone but Blondie.*

*"Let's not discuss fees for the moment. I prefer to think of this as an opportunity for mutual support, rather than a crass commercial transaction."*

*"Crass and commercial is how I rock."*

*"Give it a moment... I believe we have some enemies in common. Are you familiar with the Center for Applied Technology?"*

*Blondie's body stiffened. "That bastard Lensky uses them for cover. And his little bitch girlfriend is involved somehow too. It's damn near impossible to find out more than that."*

*"For you, possibly. I... have other resources." The speaker raised one smooth hand and his rings flashed despite the shadows. An oversized grackle fluttered out*

of the curtains and landed on his arm with a screech. Strange pet to have in a hotel.

"My friends have been paying particular attention to this Center for some time. It appears to be flourishing; from a dubious beginning with just three researchers under a doddering old professor, it now employs four and a half researchers and three support staff. The "little bitch" you mentioned is one of the researchers."

"How do you hire half a person?"

"Intern. Never mind, just listen. The Center also has the use of Bradislav Lensky, with his special connections, although he is paid directly by the agency that placed him there rather than by the Center. Possibly a distinction without a difference, since that agency also funds the Center, passing money through a research foundation to preserve their anonymity."

The bejeweled hand stroked the grackle's iridescent black feathers.

"Look," Blondie said, "if you want to pretend you're getting information from birds, fine, play it like that. I don't need to know all that about funding and staff support, I don't care about bringing down the Center. I just want to have a conversation with the two people who interfered with a multi-job deal that I was setting up last fall. They cost me a lot; I want to make them pay for it."

"My sentiments exactly, except that I am more ambitious than you. I want to see the entire Center pay for what they did to me."

"Which was?"

"You don't need to know. All you need concern yourself with is that I am in a position to offer material support and inside information… if you take out the entire Center."

"You want every employee dead? I charge by the item for hit jobs."

"What would you call your plans for Lensky and his girl?"

"Personal satisfaction."

"Very well then. My personal satisfaction would lie in seeing this Center lose all power and credibility and be so damaged that it could never be revived. I don't need any particular deaths if the goal can be achieved without them, but I won't object to a certain amount of collateral damage. Focus on Lensky if you like, but ultimately I want the whole structure brought down."

"And….?"

*The dark man raised an eyebrow. "And?"*

*"My clients make a down payment of half the total fee before I start work."*

*"Since I will be paying you with support and information, that's a bit tricky to arrange. However..."*

*The bejeweled hand stroked the grackle again. "Lamashtu, may I trouble you for one of your feathers?"*

*Rings flashed in the light as the dark man dexterously twitched a long black feather free and offered it to Blondie. "Consider this a down payment. With it, you will be able to understand the speech of my servants. You may go now."*

*Blondie started to laugh, but grackles whirred down from all the curtains and ceiling corners and surrounded him, and when they dispersed he was standing in the shade of a live oak, outside the building. He shook his head. That had been some crazy dream. Too bad he hadn't dreamed anything actually useful, like how to get at his targets without endangering himself.*

*As he was walking back to his car, an oversized grackle dove to the sidewalk just in front of him. "I can watch... GRAK."*

*In his shock, he had let go of the grackle feather in his hand. The large bird grabbed the feather in its beak, flew up clumsily and pecked at his empty hand. When his fingers touched the feather, the squawking turned comprehensible again. "Fool. Did I give up a feather only for you to lose it? Be more careful." The grackle departed with a derisive flick of its wings.*

*Tucked under one of the windshield wipers of his car was a card with only two lines printed on it."Shani Chayyaputra," read the name, printed in a flowing script with extremely shiny black ink. Below that was a telephone number.*

The Blessed Prakash wasn't due to start at the Center until Monday, and that was fine with me. Lensky usually visited his sister-in-law and niece on Friday nights, and I – unless I had a really good excuse – presented myself at my parents' house for the weekly family dinner with a side of bullying and disappointment. It wasn't all bad; Mom cooked the best Greek food in Texas and her baklava was to die for. And since I'd casually mentioned Ben and Annelise's apartment-warming party on Saturday, she had probably made an extra tray of baklava for me to take to that party.

It was just the conversation that could be hard to take.

This night was particularly difficult, because my oldest brother and his wife were out of town and my second-oldest brother had claimed sickness. That left just Andros and me to take incoming fire.

Mom led off with lamentations about my letting Ben 'get away,' while Dad inserted sour comments to the effect that he'd known all along I wouldn't be able to keep a man interested. Okay, I'd kind of bought that. For the last couple of years I'd deflected some of the "marry-and-reproduce" pressure by letting them believe that Ben and I had a thing. It wasn't difficult; it would have been much harder to convince Dad that a man and a woman could be colleagues and best friends without remotely wishing for any kind of romantic connection. Even Lensky had struggled to accept that Ben was my best friend, and he was at least living in the twentieth century, if not the twenty-first. My father, who is just short of certifiably insane, still has his head in a back-country Greek village and applies those standards to every situation he encounters in modern America.

And using Ben had made it easier for me to conceal Lensky from them.

So I had to endure a certain amount of Mom's moaning about how I let a perfectly good man get away and you're not getting any younger Thalia, while Dad surmised that Annelise was prettier than me (absolutely true) and younger (by a couple of years) and a better cook (I don't know anything about her cooking skills, but if she could boil water without reading the instructions she was better than I was).

At least he didn't mention that she was *taller*. Since Dad's not exactly a giant himself, he can accept that I'm only five foot three. Or maybe it's just that "tall" isn't on the list of desirable qualities for a Greek village bride.

Andros, on the other hand, had been shooting up over the last year. At sixteen he was already a head taller than Dad, and his broad shoulders and general appearance were a testament to Mom's cooking and American orange juice. Also, he had evidently received all of the good Greek genes in our genetic lottery: tall like Mom, smooth olive skin, curly black hair and lots of it. Me, I got the hair but not the height, for which I tried not to blame Dad.

"If I didn't know better, I'd think you were a grown man already," I commented to him during a brief pause in the criticism.

"Hah! What makes a man is *acting* like a man, not shooting up tall like a weed." Dad hadn't minded Stevie and Yanni growing up to be taller than him, but Andros getting there well before eighteen did irritate him. I don't think his patriarchal self-image included being shorter and scrawnier than *all* his sons.

You'd think he would appreciate me more. I'm not taller than anybody.

But no, he had to continue his self-imposed mission of cutting Andros down. "Andros is still a schoolboy and if he doesn't shape up he'll never be anything more."

"Seems to me a sixteen-year-old *should* be a schoolboy," I snapped.

Andros twitched in his seat. "Please, Thalia," he said in a very low voice. "He just gets worse if you argue back."

Yes. I knew that for myself, it was why I hunkered down and let Dad's criticism roll over me. Now, as he launched into a diatribe about Andros' failings, I mentally slapped myself. Why couldn't I be as smart for Andros as I was for myself?

Later, over the dishes, I tried to apologize to him. (Dad, of course, was never to be seen in the kitchen unless he wanted another beer and Mom wasn't around to bring it to him. While we washed and dried, he was in the living room watching the late news.)

"It's all right, Thalia," Andros said, but his hunched shoulders told me it was very far from all right.

"Just hang in there," I told him. "When you're eighteen I'll help you get out." I might need to get a better paying job to put Andros through university, but that was a bridge I'd burn when I got there.

He didn't look any happier. "Thalia, I'm not a brain like you. I probably won't even get into the university. Besides…"

"Silly boy thinks he wants to be a soldier and get killed!" Mom announced.

"Well. That should be achievable. Becoming a soldier, I mean, not the getting killed part. You can enlist when you're eighteen, can't you?"

Andros seemed to shrink in on himself. "I want to join the Marines," he almost whispered. "But Dad says they'll never take me."

"Dad is…" Mom caught my eye and I substituted, "not an expert on military standards," for what I'd been about to say. "I think the Marines or any other branch of the military would be overjoyed to get someone like you. Tall, fit, good grades – what's not to like?"

Andros looked even unhappier but said nothing.

"I made baklava for that party of yours," Mom said, pulling off a length of plastic wrap and swathing a large tray in it. "Not that *I* think it's anything to celebrate, but at least that Mr. Southlands will see what he's losing in you!"

Dr. Verrick, of course, didn't show up at the party. He had muttered that in *his* day young people got married first and then moved in together, and given the general incompetence of his research staff he shouldn't be surprised that they got things backwards now. Then he arranged for a set of champagne flutes and several bottles of chilled champagne to be delivered on Saturday night, and informed the staff of the Center that we were to deliver ourselves at the appropriate time to the apartment-warming party.

It wasn't a bad apartment. Certainly it was a vast improvement on Ben's previous lodging, which had been about the size of a postage stamp. Apart from being larger and cleaner, well, what do you say about apartments? "It looks nice," is better than "You signed a *lease* on this?" and that sums up my social understanding.

Actually, thanks to the fact that they couldn't afford much furniture, the place looked positively roomy. The living room held a couple of beanbag chairs, a flat-screen TV, and a card table for party snacks where we gathered after duly admiring the luxury of a separate kitchen and a dining nook.

Lensky hung up our coats and Mr. M., not a fan of cold weather, slowly slithered out of my belt loops.

All right. You may have thought Mr. M. was a person, and that's more or less correct. He certainly has plenty of personality. But it's also true that he is a Babylonian turtle mage who, after the accidental destruction of his turtle shell, makes do with a prosthetic robot snake body for transportation. I know, I know, it's hard to picture. You're probably still shaking your head over my assertion that some people can do magic via just the right kind of pure mathematics visualized in just the right way. And that's a lot easier to accept than a compound complex being made up of a box turtle head and a prosthetic snake body.

A three-thousand-year old box turtle head.

Now, thanks to our robotics engineer Meadow Melendez, equipped with GPS, wi-fi, and focused ultrasonic beam capability.

Well, I can't help it. Mr. M. *exists*. He survived a beheading that freed him from a magic-quenching ring, persuaded Meadow to give him one of her spare robot snake bodies, and has since impressed the force of his personality on everyone associated with the Center for Applied Technology. Without him we wouldn't have had nearly so many dramatic applications of topology. As I've mentioned, his infinite set of "stars" allowed serious amplification of the results we got from applying topology to problems. Each research fellow of the Center now has a personal infinite set of stars. (See, that's a very practical use of mathematics. Half of an infinite set is… an infinite set. We could keep subdividing the stars forever without running out.) We owed him a lot… and he liked to party. Naturally I brought him along.

The fact that nearly half our staff now consisted of non-mathematicians saved the party. Instead of a huddle of topologists staring at their shoes, we had topologists intermixed with Jimmy, Meadow, Lensky, and, of course, Annelise. We still stared at our shoes to begin with, of course, but after enough champagne had flowed we began to act almost normally party-ish.

I asked Meadow if she'd come up with any interesting augmentations for Mr. M. She grinned and said we'd see in due course, but what she planned to do next was a fan-(obscenity)-tastic augmentation and she felt sorry for the next bunch of (blasphemy) terrorists who had the bad judgment to tangle with the greatest warrior snake-turtle in the (extremely coarse obscenity) history of the turtle race.

Colton looked unhappy. "Why do you always talk like that, Meadow? You're much too pretty to talk so ugly."

"I am *not* pretty," she snapped, "and it's none of your (obscenity) business how I (expletive deleted) talk." Actually, she wasn't bad-looking, but 'pretty' wasn't part of her self-image. Her way of dealing with being a short Hispanic woman in a department full of engineering students was to adopt the personality of a tank, and she had the build to do it – especially given her choice of loose, bulky sweaters that did what they could to conceal her figure.

Extreme self-confidence was a feature, not a bug, in her case; without it, she'd never have dared to attempt joining Mr. M's severed head to a snake-robot body. Not only that, she kept augmenting the capabilities of that body.

I edged away from them before Colton could say anything nice to her again; I didn't want to be anywhere close to the potential explosion.

Lensky was being as useless as a mathematician at this party, or at least as quiet as one; he hardly spoke at all and barely touched the snacks. Mostly he leaned against the wall and stared into his glass.

"Have you noticed how many grackles there are around Allandale House lately?" I asked Ben. It was something of a *non sequitur*, I'm not good at small talk. Neither are any of the other researchers, of course.

Ben, for instance, took that as an invitation to explain to me that there really weren't that many grackles, they were just more conspicuous because most of the other birds in Austin had sensibly gone south. Furthermore, since they weren't breeding at this season, they had nothing much to do but wheel in the sky and perch in the trees over open areas like the South Mall or the grounds of Allandale House. Their habits…

Ben double-majored in mathematics and biology, and he hasn't quite recovered from the biology part. I slithered away from that monologue on the excuse of getting another glass of champagne. I waved brightly at Lensky from the kitchen counter that had been designated as a temporary bar, emptied my glass as soon as I caught his eye, and refilled it.

There was definitely something wrong with the man. He was passing up an opportunity to interfere with me having another drink. Despite the fact that I'm only five foot three and about ninety pounds, I can actually have more than one glass of champagne without becoming falling-down drunk, but Lensky has some trouble grasping that concept.

Ingrid looked unhappy too. I poured a second glass of champagne and shimmied along the wall until I reached her.

"You look as though you need something to drown your sorrows."

"Oh. It's nothing." Ingrid emptied the champagne flute in one gulp and handed it back to me. The braids wrapped around her head seemed to be trying to escape; when she wasn't holding a glass, she kept absent-mindedly trying to poke hairpins back into her coronet of silvery fair hair.

After a second bout of champagne therapy, she complained to me that Jimmy was being weird about her new project.

"Flying? But it's not just you, it's all of us. Well, you and Colton are doing most of the work."

"But it'll never be Jimmy," Ingrid said morosely. "Up to now he's been okay about the fact that I can do some things he can't, but..."

"He's always thought the stuff you could do was *beyond* cool." This shift in his attitude surprised me. "I should have thought he'd find flying even cooler than our other stuff."

"He doesn't like me working so much with Colton," Ingrid blurted. "He got upset because I was so excited that we've actually managed to get in the air for a few seconds."

"You have? Congratulations!"

"Apparently Jimmy doesn't share that feeling. Remember how Lensky was about you and Ben last fall?"

"To be fair, he had some excuse for leaping to his conclusions, mistaken though they were. As far as I know, Jimmy hasn't discovered you and Colton sleeping in the same bed. However innocently," I added just to make sure she remembered that there'd been nothing going on with Ben and me except exhaustion after a harrowing ordeal.

Ingrid shoved a few more escaping hairpins back into her pile of blonde braids. "All the same...Thalia, *you're* in a committed relationship with an outsider. How do you make it work?"

"The first step," Jimmy said, behind her, "is agreeing that you *are* committed to the relationship. I haven't heard a lot from you about that. And these days all I hear about is how much you want to do the aerial waltz with that farm boy."

Sheesh. If *Colton* made him jealous, I wondered what his reaction to

Prakash would be. As our resident computer nerd, rather than a research fellow, he hadn't been exposed to the Blessed Prakash yet.

Ingrid turned faintly pink around the edges. "Jimmy, not here!"

"Reassure me," Jimmy said.

"How?"

"We could be engaged, for a start. Or better, married. Unless you're too chicken to make a commitment."

Ingrid patted her braids. I had the feeling that she was mentally putting on her horned helmet. "I am not afraid of *anything*!" she announced in ringing tones. "I'm not afraid of flying, I'm not afraid of you, and I'm certainly not afraid to make a commitment!"

"Great! We'll get married at spring break!"

"June. If we're getting married, you have something else to do over spring break."

"I do?"

Ingrid's smile had some elements of the shark sensing blood. "Meeting my mother. Again."

She swanned off towards the champagne while Jimmy turned so pale green that all his freckles stood out. It wasn't a good look for him. But I could understand. He'd met Ingrid's mother once before, as a colleague rather than as a future husband, and he'd said it was one of those occasions when your whole life passes before your eyes.

Hmm. I had the feeling I'd just watched somebody being very adroitly manipulated. The only question was, which one of them had been doing the manipulating?

I still hadn't made up my mind on that when Mr. M. decided to serenade the happy couple with "You'd Be So Nice to Come Home to." It would have been OK if he'd stopped there. But he went on to give us a bravura interpretation of "Beer Barrel Polka," followed by "Der Führer's Face" – complete with raspberries, and how a being with a beak instead of lips could do that is something I don't want to think about. Last fall he'd been into sentimental nineteenth century songs; now he'd moved on to the Big Band era and the second world war. In a sense this was progress; if he kept moving forward in time, he'd eventually get to classic rock, music I actually liked.

Then again, I'm not sure the world is ready for a turtle head with a synthetic snake body belting out, "Sharp Dressed Man."

"Did anybody give him coffee?" I whispered to Ingrid. Caffeine had a known effect on Mr. M.; that's why we tried to keep it away from him. But I hadn't seen any coffee at this party.

She shook her head. "But I think Annelise poured some champagne in a saucer for him. She said something about not wanting him to feel left out."

"That girl is too tender-hearted for her own good. Or maybe for my own good. She gets him drunk and I have to take him home and get him to sleep."

"You could leave him here."

Mr. M. sounded ready to go for the rest of the night. I was tempted. Sorely tempted. But when Lensky held my coat, he stopped singing to squawk, slither across the floor, and start working up my leg. I was wearing a skirt, so I picked him up before this got too intimate. He coiled himself around my waist, hiccupping and asserting that he was the Boogie-Woogie Bugle Boy of Company C.

By the time we got home he was asleep.

# 5. I do not even wish to know that it exists

"Okay, give. All evening you've been looking like somebody stole your ice cream cone. What's the matter? I'd have thought you'd be delighted that Ben and Annelise were moving in together."

"I'm happy for them, hope it works out well," Lensky said, so mechanically that it was clear his mind was on something quite different.

"You're not even thinking about them. What's bothering you?"

He sighed heavily and began unlacing his shoes. "Thalia, you know there are aspects of my work that I can't share with you."

I pulled my silk shirt over my head and stepped out of my skirt. Lensky didn't even look up. And here I was wearing a new camisole and knickers set, silk with lace inserts. Kind of a deep rose color. And apparently wasted on this occasion. "Is this one of those aspects? Tell me straight out that whatever's worrying you is too classified for me to hear about, and I'll quit bugging you." If only because I couldn't think of anything else to do.

Lensky has problems with telling me a direct lie. That would seem to be a bug, not a feature, for somebody working for an agency so secretive that he wasn't supposed to say its name; but when I asked him about it once he said that it was only me he had trouble lying to, he didn't have any problem lying to the idiots and lowlifes he recruited as informants.

Well, a girl likes to feel special. But now I was exploiting my "special" status to pressure Lensky, and I didn't much like myself for that.

It worked, though. He met my eyes and sighed. "No, in fact the Agency has been leaning on me to enlist the Center's help on this, and - I don't like it. I don't want you anywhere near this. Just because you've seen him…"

"It's about Blondie."

"Yes. I told you there'd been chatter placing him in Austin? Now one of my assets has linked him with an Austin businessman, says they've met at the bar in the Driskill more than once recently. Of course he, the informant, hasn't actually seen Blondie. He's going on that sketch our people put together after San Antonio. To verify the connection, they - we - would like somebody who would recognize Blondie to have a look at one of these meetings. I can…"

"You can *not* waltz off and try to surveil Blondie!" I interrupted. "It's too dangerous. He knows what you look like now!"

"If my theories about having crossed his path in Romania are correct, he's known that for several years."

"Doesn't make it any safer for you now."

"I've been trying to persuade my asset to take pictures next time, but he doesn't have the nerve. He's heard - stories - about what Blondie does to people who cross him."

"Well, there's a much easier solution." Here was a chance to actually be of some real help to Lensky, using known applications of topology. "Have your asset phone me next time he sees Blondie. I'll teleport to the hotel, raise Camouflage as soon as I'm there, and observe. If it is Blondie… well, I don't know whether I can take a picture of his companion through Camouflage, I need to run some tests."

"Confirmation that it's Blondie will be all we need, we already know who the other guy is," Lensky said absently, "Shani Chayyaputra, new in town, venture capitalist, something to do with computers…wait a minute. You can't do this either, Thalia. He knows what you look like."

"So what?" I said. "He won't even see me. No wonder the Agency's been leaning on you; this is exactly the kind of little thing where our special abilities can be most effective. Don't you see? You can't verify that it's Blondie, because he might see you. Your informant can't verify him beyond saying he looks like the sketch, and we both know it's not so great." The artist had captured Blondie's close-cropped pale blond hair, his cold gray eyes and thin nose, but had somehow failed to convey the tension and sense of danger that Blondie radiated. "But I can verify safely, using Camouflage. He'll never even know I was there."

"Right, he won't... because you won't be there. I'm not letting you do this."

There's a point at which there's just no use arguing with Lensky any longer. It's like his mind turns into quick-setting cement. So I didn't push it then. I worried, though. Because I felt sure that Lensky would want to observe the next meeting between Blondie and the other guy, and although I could have done so safely, he would be in danger. His Agency had probably taught him all sorts of little tricks for being inconspicuous and not easily recognizable, but all those tricks put together wouldn't be nearly as good as the cloak of invisibility I could throw over myself.

Perhaps I could persuade him to take one of the other topologists to the Driskill. That way, with somebody holding Camouflage over the two of them, he could observe the meeting as safely as I could have.

Or perhaps I could go at the problem from a different angle.

On Monday we got our first experience of working with Prakash. If you can call it working. He kept interrupting our attempts to explain and demonstrate our abilities to talk about how much mathematics he knew, how well he'd done at the Tata Institute and his triumphs before that at the Delhi branch of the Indian Institute for Technology. We hadn't yet heard about how he aced the IIT entrance exams, but I felt sure that was coming soon.

"He's intolerably condescending," I griped to Colton Edwards during a quiet moment in the break room.

"I think he's terrified," Colton said thoughtfully. "If his own paranormal activities were enough to throw him into total denial, how much more frightening must it be to get tossed in with us? I expect he's afraid that if he lets us get a word in edgewise, we'll present him with evidence that he can't deny."

"There you go again, making the rest of us look bad by being such a nice guy. Are you going to take the last apple fritter?"

"Do you think I'm such a nice guy that I'll give it to you? I'm not *that* obliging," said Colton, cramming the thing into his mouth.

While he was chewing, I asked if he had any suggestions for reducing Prakash's putative terror.

"He barely knows us," Colton said after he finished off the apple fritter. "Why don't we invite him to join us for lunch? Maybe he'll relax a little in an informal setting."

It was, thus, entirely Colton's fault that the four of us were breathing fire after lunch that day. Instead of grabbing a sandwich or burger at the Student Union, we'd walked a few blocks down Guadalupe to a combination Indian restaurant and grocery store that Prakash liked.

"Recommendations?" Ben asked him.

"Everything here is good," Prakash said, "but I am vegetarian, so I can personally recommend vegetarian dishes only. I suggest you request special mild version of whatever you order. Indian food is very spicy."

"We all trained on jalapeño nachos," Ben said, "that won't be an issue."

Seldom has there been such a wildly inaccurate prediction. And yes, I'm including the TV weatherman who kept promising a cold front all through last August.

Slightly less than an hour later, we were back on the Drag; four topologists taking deep gasps of the nice cool January air, and one shivering but smug intern. "So, how you are liking Indian food?"

"I *think* it was pretty good," Ben said, "but honestly, all I could taste most of the time was *hot*. I mean, the impression that your mouth, throat and sinuses have been attacked by a flamethrower makes it hard to concentrate on the subtleties of flavor and texture. Next time I'll follow your recommendation, Prakash, and beg them to make it mild for the innocent American."

We crossed Guadalupe and started walking down 21st.

"This is not shortest way back to Allandale House," Prakash pointed out. He was wearing a jacket over a pullover over a button-down shirt and was still shivering. The rest of us hadn't bothered to bring jackets; it was over sixty degrees and sunny today, and long sleeves were all we really needed.

"Slight detour," Ben said. "I want to know what that is, don't you?"

"That" appeared to be a minor carnival put on by utility workers. There were flashing lights and random bangs and squeaks and there was a lot of pointing up at the trees over Littlefield Fountain.

"No," said Prakash, stalled by his first good look at the fountain. "I do not wish to know what that is. I do not even wish to know that it exists."

"It's not as bad as the Albert Memorial in London," Ingrid told him.

"Albert Memorial is *in* London, and I am not anticipating having to see it regularly. This is…"

His voice trailed off, and he appeared to be temporarily at a loss for words.

I could sympathize. The designer of Littlefield Fountain had approached the concept of "war memorial" with surprising exuberance. The bronze horses with their webbed front feet rearing up out of the spray weren't bad exactly, but their nude, pointy-eared riders began to seem like too much of a good thing. And the larger-than-life-size winged goddess riding some kind of spiral thingie behind them did stress the eyeballs some. She appeared to be brandishing a torch in one hand and something that might have been a palm leaf in the other, and I'd always been impressed by her ability to balance up there with both hands full. Throw in the naked sailor on one side (identifiable by his hat) and the naked soldier on the other (identifiable by his helmet) and you had the beginnings of something that could give the Albert Memorial a run for its money.

But hey, it's our fountain, and we love it. Sort of.

At least once each winter some students express their love by dumping detergent into the fountain. The resulting cascade of soap bubbles looks as if the fountain's been in a snowstorm. Sort of.

That was what I'd expected to see today, but the fountain was clear and the folks in dark blue uniforms who were running the circus appeared to be more interested in the live oaks overhead.

A series of bangs happened much closer to my ears than I was comfortable with, and a small cloud of grackles took off from the trees, jeered, and settled farther up the mall. Meanwhile, Ben had corralled one of the uniformed people and was getting her explanation for what was going on. I'm sure it was purely coincidence that he'd corralled the only worker with long hair and perfume.

"Alamo Bird Services," she said, "doing grackle dispersal. We shoot cap guns, bang blocks of wood together, and blind them with lasers." She tapped the strange black instrument on her hip. "This thing is kind of like a giant light saber. The lights hit the birds in the eyes and they can't understand what it is, it makes them nervous, eventually they decide they're rather be somewhere else."

"So all you're doing, really," Ingrid said, "is shuffling grackles from one area to another."

Ms. Bird Services shrugged. "It's a Federal crime to kill grackles. Migratory Bird Treaty of 1918."

Ingrid paled, probably remembering the number of dead grackles she'd left behind her at the Battle of Mayfield Park.

"Don't worry if you've killed some," Ms. Bird Services said. "The Feds actually have some sense; they don't go after frustrated homeowners who may have cleared the trees above their driveway with a shotgun. But if *we* started killing grackles it would be hard for them to overlook it. So the policy is startle, don't kill. And yes, it is just moving them from one area to another. But we find it only takes about three days to clear a bunch this size, and then the grackles don't come back to the same spot for a year, year and a half. Excuse me."

Black birds were settling on the branches overhead. She unsheathed her light saber and used it like a demented eight-year-old with a flashlight, whirling it in wild, wobbly circles while the birds croaked in protest.

Ben asked her a question that was half drowned out by a new salvo from the cap guns squad.

"Yes, we've contracted to do the entire west campus. We'll get up to the Allandale House area eventually. Not for a while; we're working south to north."

"That," said Ben when his new friend had gone back to de-grackling the trees, "is interesting and potentially very useful."

"Interesting, yes, but I do not see any usefulness." Prakash had been fixated on the fountain all this time, ignoring the activities of Alamo Bird Services. "Why the men riding on the horses are having pointed ears? And what is wrong with front hooves of horses?"

"The horses must be kelpies," Colton said, "and the riders…" He shrugged. "I dunno. Elves?"

"Why in a war memorial? What are elves and kelpies having to do with war? And cannot we return to office now?"

To the accompaniment of Prakash's intermittent whining, we strolled up the South Mall and then over to Allandale House. When we got there, Ben grabbed Mr. M. out of my office and went back to the public side to confer with Meadow. To give him credit, he had thought of an excellent augmentation for Mr. M., not that we got to see it right away.

By the time Ben got out of his conference with Meadow, Prakash had taken himself off. He claimed unfinished business with the mathematics department, but I suspected he just wanted to get away from us. Well, fine; the feeling was mutual. Besides, I wanted to talk to Ben about Blondie and the Driskill.

# 6. A job for the Center

"It's a job for the Center that Lensky won't let the Center do," I told Ben once he was back on the private side of the office. As long as we kept our voices down, we were safe from Lensky overhearing us; his office was on the public side and he couldn't cross the wall without help. I updated Ben on the current state of the Blondie problem and the need to verify that he was the person who'd been meeting this Shani Chayyaputra in the bar at the Driskill. Which, of course, I could have done with no problems but no, instead we were going to have to come at this backwards and upside-down.

Then again, backwards and upside-down is exactly how we've achieved some of our greatest successes.

"Lensky is being an over-protective idiot again," I finished. "He wants to do something that will actually be risky for him – not to mention alerting his target – instead of letting me do it in perfect safety using your Camouflage algorithm."

Ben looked alarmed. "Look, Thalia, I'm not getting between you and Lensky *ever again*. I'm still surprised he didn't kill me back when that thing happened in October."

"Oh, it was me he wanted to kill," I said.

"And as I recall, he damned near succeeded. I don't ever want to see you looking like that again, either."

"Well, never mind that now. It was just a stupid misunderstanding. Anyway, I wasn't going to ask you to make him change his mind. I doubt that

41

MARGARET BALL

you could. No, I was thinking that we might approach the problem from a different angle. He let slip the name of the guy Blondie's been seen with. If we can find out more about him, maybe find out the nature of his connection with Blondie, then there might be no need for anyone to observe their next meeting." I told him what little Lensky had said about Shani Chayyaputra.

"And if you don't mention this bright idea to Lensky, he can't forbid you to do it."

"Well, yes, that too. Better to ask forgiveness than permission, and all that. Any way, he is not the boss of me. He has zero authority to dictate what I do as a research fellow of the Center."

"I just hope he sees it that way," Ben said gloomily. "Oh, well… you say this Chayyaputra's CEO of a startup in the computer business? Why don't we start by asking Jimmy to do a little informal research? Lensky can hardly object to that."

Ben walked Jimmy back to our side so that he could explain what we needed without being overheard, and I let him work in my office so that he could search without the risk of Lensky noticing. The first results were not impressive. "I can't find any business filings under that name. In fact, I can't find anything at all except that there's a Chayyaputra registered at the Driskill Hotel."

"That's him! Has to be; that explains why Blondie's been meeting him in the bar. If it is Blondie."

"Who's Blondie, his girlfriend?"

"Not hardly!" I explained what we knew, or thought we knew, or suspected, about Blondie and his possible relationship with Chayyaputra.

"An owner of a computer-related startup would have no legitimate business with a bomb expert," Ben mused. "It sure would be interesting to know what Chayyaputra's *really* doing here."

"Whatever it is," Jimmy said, "it's not under his name, and I don't know where else to look. I need some kind of a starting point."

At this point Ben's phone rang and he almost fell off his chair grabbing it.

"It's Annelise," he said, "bearing more doughnuts. I'll just go and walk her in." Since the crises of last fall, Annelise seemed to have decided that topologists need doughnuts the way normal people need oxygen. This time we hadn't been depleting our blood sugar by teleporting or flying, but thinking this hard seemed to have a similar effect; the chocolate-covered ones looked especially good to me.

She set the tray down and asked why we were looking so gloomy. Ben summarized our progress and the point at which we'd gotten stuck.

"Well, that's easy enough!" Annelise said. "The trouble with you folks is, you've forgotten there were ever any simple and natural ways to do anything. If you can't do it by hacking into a computer, or teleporting to foreign parts, or making yourselves invisible, you think it can't be done at all."

"Technically," Ben said, "we never have teleported to 'foreign parts.' West Texas just *seems* like another country."

"What did you have in mind?" I asked Annelise.

She dimpled. "Well, men just naturally like to talk to a pretty girl. Give them any encouragement at all and you can't hardly shut them up. Single man, staying at the Driskill? I bet he's down at that bar every night. He'll tell me whatever we want to know."

"Won't he be suspicious? I mean, why would somebody like you let some strange man at a bar pick her up?"

"Single man, staying at the Driskill? R-I-C-H," Annelise said succinctly. "Not as rich as Daddy, of course, but rich enough to attract the wrong sort of girl."

Ben shook his head. "Annelise, you can't do it, it's too dangerous. I won't let you!"

Annelise's chin stuck out. "I don't recall asking your permission!"

A nasty squabble was averted when Jimmy bravely jumped into the argument. "She has a point, Ben. I don't see why those of us who lack paranormal abilities should be left out of everything. Look, you can be there too; sit in a corner, nurse a drink, keep your eye on things. If it looks like it's going bad, you can grab Annelise and teleport back to your apartment."

We spent some time working over the details. None of us had actually seen Chayyaputra. Jimmy would get his room number and Ben would lurk outside the room, camouflaged, until he got a good look at the man. Then he'd take position in the bar, Annelise would come in and ignore him, and when – if – Chayyaputra came in, Ben would signal her.

It occurred to me, tardily, that Annelise ought to have some idea what Blondie looked like. What if she accidentally witnessed his next meeting with Chayyaputra? Maybe I should be in the bar too, so that I could warn her.

Ben nixed that. "You'd have to be camouflaged the entire time, Thalia, and you *know* how hard it is to maintain Camouflage in a public place with all kinds of people milling around. Besides, Lensky will kill me if I let you join us there."

I couldn't argue with him about that.

Perhaps I could get a copy of that sketch Lensky's agency had made up based on our descriptions of the man. It wasn't a *great* likeness, but it was better than nothing – especially, I realized, since Lensky's informant had ID'd Blondie on that basis. I mean, Chayyaputra's drinking buddy might or might not be Blondie, but he was definitely somebody who resembled that sketch.

For now, I just gave Annelise the thumbnail version: "Tall. Slender. Short blond hair, almost a crewcut. Gray eyes – *scary* gray eyes," I added, remembering the one time I'd stood face to face with him. "Um, tense, menacing. Almost certainly carries."

"Tall and blond?" Annelise repeated. "Oh – oh, I've just had a *brilliant* idea! Why don't I let Chayyaputra ask me out?"

"Let him pick you up, you mean?" Ben sounded less than thrilled with this notion.

Annelise ignored him. "I'll tell him I never go out without my roomie, but if he can come up with somebody for her we'll double-date."

"Roomie?"

"I've got a picture of Ingrid and me on my phone. I'll explain that she only goes out with guys who are taller than her, and she only likes blonds."

That sounded awfully flimsy to me. "Do you really think he'll fall for that?"

"This is *Annelise* you're talking to, Thalia," Ben said. "She can make anybody believe anything. Remember how she talked us out of that little mess in Mayfield Park last spring?"

"Little" mess? Exploded water moccasin, mysteriously dead grackles falling out of the sky, shots fired, killer snakebot on the warpath?

"I retract my doubts." I still wasn't thrilled with putting other people out on the sharp end, but I had to admit: Annelise could make anybody believe anything.

And if the "double-date" ploy worked, we could confirm Blondie's identity there and then.

***

Ben spent an extremely boring afternoon camouflaging himself as the wallpaper on the fifth floor of the Driskill before he spotted Shani Chayyaputra exiting his hotel room, and then he and Annelise staked out the bar for two nights with no sight of Chayyaputra. It was an *extremely* pricey place, and I wasn't even getting any drinks for my money.

"You're not missing much," Annelise told me after that second night. "I ordered their special Austin cocktail, the Batini."

"They serve that other times than Bat Fest?" Austin makes a big deal out of the bats who come swooping out from under bridges in the fall. Never understood it, myself. But then, perhaps my experiences with grackles have prejudiced me against clouds of flying black animals that poop on your head.

"Unfortunately, yes." Annelise made a face. "Their version involves cucumber, lemongrass-infused vodka, and Blue Curacao sherbert."

"Sorbet," Ben said automatically.

"Whatever. I'd rather have a beer."

I'd rather she had a beer too. The drinks fund was running low.

We decided to give it one more night.

That was Wednesday morning. Before lunch, Lensky gave us reason to change that decision.

# 7. Intelligent, competent, angry and amoral

"Start with this," Lensky said. "His real name is Sandru Balan." He looked abstracted for a minute. "Balan... hmm. After Thalia and I glimpsed him last fall we assumed his nickname was because of his blond hair. But it could also be a play on his name; in Romanian *Balan* means "blond." As I told Thalia, those scraps of paper we recovered from his hotel safe have been the occasion of a prolonged party for our translators and analysts. Not to mention giving the FBI something useful to do for once."

He had collected the entire research staff of the Center for Applied Technology – Prakash excepted - to brief us on his agency's discoveries about the terrorist we'd known only as "Blondie." He'd persuaded the agency that in this case, keeping information strictly compartmented was less important than making sure everybody who might be at risk was on the same page.

We were crowded into my office on the private side of the third floor. Not for the first time, I considered the success of Ben's visitor-discouraging strategy (have an office the size of a walk-in closet) versus mine (don't have any chairs for visitors). Oh, well. This wasn't a casual visit; it was a semi-formal meeting after which, I hoped, the other research fellows would go back to their own offices and take their chairs with them. We usually had meetings in the break room, on the public side, but Lensky was antsy about sharing so much of the intelligence his agency had gathered. It had seemed best to walk him across the wall and meet here, where nobody could casually eavesdrop.

Unlike Lensky, though, I wasn't too worried about that possibility. The number of people who want to eavesdrop on mathematicians' conversations is vanishingly small. Even the Center's support staff tended to back away, muttering about crosses and garlic, when we got into a lively discussion about, say, finitely generated vector spaces.

Granted, the present briefing was somewhat more user-friendly than that.

"We have a lot more information about Balan now, and we're not even through analyzing all the papers that were retrieved last fall. Not just his identity, but birth date, early life, skills, and some interesting theories about his motivations."

"I thought you knew the last part," Ben said. "Isn't he a jihadi? Or is that too politically incorrect to mention?"

"We thought that at one time," Lensky said, "but with the benefit of more data, we're back to the theory that he's a mercenary who is willing to sell his skills to the highest bidder."

"But a lot of his notes were written in Arabic, weren't they?" Ingrid asked. "I wouldn't think many Romanians would know Arabic."

"They wouldn't." Lensky looked as if he'd bitten into a lemon. "Balan, however, is highly intelligent and particularly talented with languages. We believe that he assumed the persona of a radicalized American and even taught himself Arabic in order to infiltrate the group he was dealing with last fall. That would have been an extremely lucrative contract, involving major bombings across the country. San Antonio, Albuquerque, Denver and Los Angeles were definitely targeted. We believe there were also plans for Dallas, Tucson, and San Francisco."

I closed my eyes for a moment. "You did say *were?*"

"Based on information in Balan's papers, the FBI was able to pick up several key members of the group. They moved on different cells simultaneously and believe that they've permanently broken up that particular terrorist group."

"FBI?" Ingrid said. "But I thought you were – "

"The Agency," Lensky interrupted her. "has limited law-enforcement authority. If we identify someone who should be arrested, we notify local LEOs or the FBI." He had that sour-lemon expression again. Given his opinion of the FBI, it really galled him to have to cede to their authority. I had known better than to raise the subject; Ingrid, of course, had never had the learning experience of sitting beside Lensky while he watched a TV show about espionage and law enforcement and shouted insults at the scriptwriters. Many of the insults were also slurs on the competence of the FBI, NSA, and any other members of the intelligence community apart from his own agency.

"Why do you think he's not ideological?" I asked, just to change the subject.

"Pattern of behavior," Lensky said. "He's now been linked to bombings carried out by ETA – Basque separatists – as well as some purely commercial ventures. We know he consulted with Lashkar-e-Taiba before the Mumbai attacks in '08, but that's the only incident before last fall that can be definitely linked with both Balan and Islamist ideology. And at that time he wasn't posing as a jihadi. We presume he learned Arabic in order to insert himself into Islamist terror groups, because let's face it, nowadays that's where the money is for, um, independent contractors like Balan. But with any luck, last fall's arrests will have destroyed his credibility with his terrorist buddies. If we got *really* lucky, they'd kill him themselves, but sadly, that hasn't happened. Yet."

"I can't believe anybody would contract to maim and kill innocent people just for money," Ingrid said.

"What, you think it's less evil if they maim and kill innocents because they don't like the color of their skin, or their religion, or their laws?" Lensky was getting testy. "I can tell you this about Balan: he'll take a contract for anywhere, any time, if there's enough money in it to balance the risk for him. He literally does not care whom he kills. Oh, did I mention he's also carried out targeted political and commercial assassinations? Apparently he has sniper skills as well as demolition expertise."

"But... how does a person *get* that way?"

"He was born in Romania," Lensky said. "In 1982. Probably. The exact birth date isn't known, but he was definitely in one of the state orphanages by 1985, and they estimated that he was three years old then."

Ingrid frowned. "But just because somebody was in an orphanage doesn't make them a bad person."

"No, thank God," Lensky said, "but the worst ones can be soul-destroying. Romanian orphanages were notoriously terrible – they just warehoused the children. Rooms full of children tied to their cribs so they wouldn't make trouble for the caretakers, adolescents in straitjackets… they were nightmare places. The truth about them came out after the collapse of the Soviet Empire, but many of them kept operating after that because, well, Romania was broke, and there was no other place for the children.

"Many of the children in orphanages were physically or mentally undeveloped, some permanently. Our analysts surmise that Balan escaped those fates by pouring all his energy, first, into developing his intellect, and second, into dominating his caretakers and the other children so that he, at least, was adequately fed. He ran away from the orphanage in his early teens and probably spent some time living on the streets.

"He did not, however, escape all the effects of the orphanage. Many of the children displayed some signs of reactive attachment disorder – an inability to connect emotionally or to maintain relationships. Balan appears to be an extreme case: no personal relationships, no sense of guilt, no values, unable to trust…"

Lensky threw up his hands. "Short version: he has no moral center and, probably, no authentic feelings except one."

"And what is that one?" Ben asked.

"Anger." Lensky looked around the room, focusing his gaze on each of us in turn. "This is a very intelligent, very competent man with absolutely no qualms about hurting others and with a great deal of anger against the world. He is extremely dangerous and I don't want any of you trying to "help" by prying into his affairs. In fact, should any of you come into contact with him, do *not* engage. Just notify me and I'll take it from there." He looked at me. "Thalia, if I'd known all this last fall, I would never have enlisted your help with him. I hope you can see now why I don't want you trying to identify him or having any contact whatsoever with him."

Ben and I carefully refrained from looking at each other until Lensky had gone back to his office on the public side.

"That's it," I said. "He must never know what you and Annelise were doing the last two nights. And you certainly can't do it again."

Ben sighed. "It does seem a pity." But he didn't argue.

Annelise, however, had a different opinion when we talked to her.

"I've already spent two evenings in that bar, drinking bad cocktails and swatting bored businessmen away. Now you want to *quit* before we get any *results?*"

We had gone out for lunch to compare notes in privacy and well away from Lensky. And a good thing, too, because her voice was rising with every word.

"It's too dangerous," Ben said.

"It isn't any more dangerous than it was yesterday!"

"We didn't know all this about Blon – Balan – yesterday."

"So? We already knew he cosied up to terrorists to help them bomb places. We already knew he was dangerous enough that Lensky was spooked about letting Lia get close enough to identify him. *And,*" Annelise finished with what she evidently thought was a clinching argument, "we're not even spying on Bl – Balan. We're checking out some guy who might or might not have met him."

"Not any more, we aren't," Ben said. "I won't let you take the risk."

"Then I'll just have to do it on my own."

"Without me to point out Chayyaputra, you *can't* do it. And I'm not cooperating."

That sounded to me like the effective end of the argument. Annelise was flushed and her hair was curling crisply around her face and she hadn't given up quite yet, but obviously she wasn't going to get anywhere. I excused myself to go back to my nice quiet office – and to spare myself listening to the two of them bickering.

Therefore, I don't know exactly how Annelise turned a flat refusal to continue spying on Chayyaputra into an agreement that they'd give it one more night. *And* into an agreement not to talk to me about it until afterwards.

"You should know how it's done," Lensky said, later, when we were confessing all to him. "You do it to me all the time."

Do I?

Oh, well, maybe just once or twice I've taken the obvious and logical steps to resolve a situation without going into details with him beforehand. But that's different. I think.

Anyway, I didn't know about Ben and Annelise until the next day, and by that time they'd been through so much that they may have forgotten some details of how it all started.

*** 

In any case, all I was worried about that afternoon was not killing Prakash Bhatia. *Continuing* to not kill him. After hiding out in the math department library all morning, he'd come back to Allandale House to continue his mission of being the most irritating person in the known world. He didn't need to continue that campaign; he already had my vote.

He was still (a) refusing to admit that any use of topology could generate paranormal effects, and (b) telling us how much more topology he knew than any of us and how many distinguished mathematicians had been associated with the Tata Institute. I wasn't the only person who quietly wished that he'd take himself back to the wonderful Tata Institute. But I was the one who was stuck with him on this bright, crisp January afternoon; we'd been handing him off according to an informal rota so that nobody would go mad from dealing with him for too long, and it was my turn.

I just hadn't realized that he would discover yet a third way to be annoying.

That afternoon I was trying to talk him through a very minor visualization, kind of hoping that the exercise would settle the Matter of Prakash one way or the other. Either he'd succeed in a minor selection, understand his abilities, and have an instant breakthrough; or he'd fail so comprehensively and thoroughly that we'd feel justified in handing him back to Dr. Verrick with a report that his buried talent was buried so deep that it would take a crew of mining engineers to unearth it.

Okay, just call me a cockeyed optimist. To date the topologists of the Center had a zero success rate at either (a) getting through Prakash's blocks or (b) changing Dr. Verrick's mind about anything whatsoever. But I, being so very clever, was going to achieve one of those things this very afternoon?

Well, no. But I did give it my best shot.

"Let's work on the Axiom of Choice today," I told Prakash.

He looked down his perfectly sculpted nose at me. "Kid stuff."

"Yes, so even you -" Stop. Swallow rejoinder. Back up. Restart. "I thought it might help to work on something both of us are perfectly clear on."

"For every collection S of mutually disjoint non-empty sets there exists a set S' containing one and only one element of each set in S," he rattled off in one breath. "What is there to work on?"

"Well… what do you see when you think about the Axiom of Choice?"

Another sneer. "At this moment I am seeing a girl who pretends to be a serious mathematician, sitting in an exceedingly untidy office."

Maybe the man had a death wish.

I took a couple of deep breaths and wished we had discovered a visualization which would endow you with preternatural calm and patience. Maybe I could get Ben to think about that; he was very creative at finding new applications of topology.

"Not what you see with your eyes," I said carefully, "what you see in your mind. When you go into your math space and think about that axiom, what do you see?"

"Math space?"

"Where you go inside your head to think about mathematics." I felt on reasonably firm ground there; Prakash wouldn't have had these troubling little incidents happening around him unless he visualized mathematical concepts the same way that all the rest of us did.

"I am not describing the inside of my head. This is meaningless babble."

"All right, then I'll do it for you. You see a dark, empty space. You populate it with glowing objects corresponding to the concepts you are thinking about. In this case, you see a collection of separate and distinct shapes, each of which turns out, when you look closely at it, to be composed of many bright points. You picture one point leaving each shape…"

"Stop!" For the first time since he'd been inflicted upon us, Prakash looked shaken. "How you are knowing this about me?"

"Because that's the way the math space in my head works," I told him, "and the way it works for all four of the research fellows. We have never found anybody with the power to connect mathematical constructs and real-world objects who *doesn't* visualize that way. Hence, if you really have the latent talent Dr. Verrick believes you have, you see things that way too."

He stood up and went to the floor-to-ceiling window that opens onto one of Allandale House's cute little balconies and that was one of my reasons for grabbing this office. At this time of year there wasn't much to look at except a tangle of tree limbs and the occasional grackle, but he seemed to be studying the view intently. He shoved his hands into the pockets of his tailored pants, balled them up into fists, yanked them out again.

"The way in which one is seeing these ideas," he said eventually, "is not important. All that matters is whether one is translating them into mathematically correct statements and rigorous proofs."

"If you're doing traditional mathematics, that's true," I agreed. "For the… ah… kind of sideways math we do here, it turns out that the way you visualize the concepts is key. Why don't you have a seat? I'd prefer not to talk to the back of your head."

"I have never desired to do anything but what you call 'traditional' maths," he said. He pulled his chair back and sat down very carefully, as if he thought something might break.

For the first time, I felt some sympathy for him. "Neither did I - once upon a time. None of us did. I mean, I'm pretty sure nobody grows up wanting to have paranormal abilities that have to be concealed from the entire rest of the world."

"I am not so sure," Prakash said. "Even in India, comic book heroes such as the Superman are much admired. But I do not wish to live in a comic book. I prefer a university."

"Well, nobody's drafting you into the Center."

"This is true."

"Do you want to get out of here and go back to working on your dissertation?"

"That is… not an option," Prakash said, surprising me. "I am here to work under supervision of your Professor Verrick, isn't it? He is of opinion that I was taking too much course work too fast at Tata Institute and must take a short pause to, he says, solidify key concepts. Mentally. He will not accept me again as dissertation candidate until end of this semester."

Much of this, of course, I'd already gathered from Dr. Verrick himself, but I hadn't expected to hear Prakash admit it. Perhaps his attitude towards us was softening.

I hoped.

Because it was going to be hell spending the entire semester with somebody who not only didn't believe in what we were doing but considered all of us except possibly Ingrid to be his intellectual inferiors.

That gave me a brilliant idea. "If you're going to be at loose ends until June... Why don't you take this chance to go home? Visit your family? There's certainly enough time." And Prakash in Bangalore or Mumbai or wherever would be a lot easier on us than Prakash on the third floor of Allandale House.

He winced slightly at this suggestion. "That... might be unwise... at this time."

I waited.

"My family is..." He came to a halt and started over. "My mother especially.... They were desiring me to marry before I left country. There is this girl... A cousin really, daughter of my father's brother, so she is quite suitable. Indeed, we grew up together. You know what is cousin-sister?"

I shook my head.

"Is what we call someone who is cousin only, but so close that she might be sister. Arushi, she is cousin-sister to me, very nice girl, but we... I... I do not wish to marry her. If I go home for visit, it will... they will expect I have come home for wedding."

I started to dislike him less, now that he was revealing a human side.

"I can relate," I said. "My own family is constantly on my case about getting married, and what's worse, they're right here in town, conveniently located for nagging and pressure."

"But is different, no? A woman should do as family tells her."

"Oh? And is Arushi happy to do as she's told, to marry a man who doesn't love her?'

"Of course. She is good girl."

# 8. A whirling cloud of grackles

"And that was where I lost it with him," I told Lensky that night. "Really. I mean, I managed to keep it together for a few more minutes, but at that point I was totally ready to kill him. And it didn't help any when he tried to justify his attitude by "explaining" that I didn't have a real profession and was just playing around with this fantasy of having paranormal powers to put off my proper task of marrying some man and giving him sons."

"Ouch," Lensky said appreciatively. "I wish you'd told me all this before we got comfortable."

"Why?"

"Well, I assume you're telling me because you want help moving the body."

I snickered. "Oh, no. I've decided that killing's too good for him. I told him to meet me at the office tomorrow night after everyone else has gone home and I'll demonstrate exactly how real the Center's work is."

"Why tomorrow night?"

"Well, you already told me you were making veal piccata tonight. I didn't want to miss that." I ran a hand over his shoulder. "I kind of wanted to see you, too."

"No, I mean why the secret meeting at night?"

I hadn't really been thinking clearly at the time; it took me a moment to figure out why that had seemed like the right thing.

"Once he has to accept that this is real, there's a chance he will choose to stay and work with us. That's what Dr. Verrick wants. And it will be easier for Prakash to make that choice if he hasn't been made to look a fool in front of the whole research division."

"Good Lord. What are you planning to do to the man? Fly him over the South Mall?"

"I haven't been able to fly yet," I said with some regret. It would be *extremely* satisfactory… "Anyway, I'd better stay with my strengths. I'm going to teleport him from one side of the third floor to the other until he concedes. If that doesn't work, maybe Ingrid and Colton can demonstrate flying on Friday. If they've solved their technical problems – I haven't heard how that's going, she said they're not going to announce anything until they can do it right. Stop hogging the covers, I'm cold."

Lensky liberated a bit of the duvet and flipped it over me. "Has it occurred to you that Bhatia may have misinterpreted your challenge?"

"How? I told him exactly what I intended to do." I rolled over with my back to him so I could warm my icy feet on his legs.

"Aargh! Why do women have such cold feet? Given what you've told me about his attitudes, he may well think that there's only one reason a young woman would arrange to be alone with him."

"Oh, don't be silly. Even Prakash couldn't have his head that far up his – I mean, be that much of a pompous idiot. He knows about you and me; it's not like he thinks I'm cruising around looking to hook up with somebody."

"All the same," Lensky said, "I think I should be there too. Just in case." His voice sounded a bit strained and I turned so that I could see his face.

"Brad, I really, really don't want you to do that. Don't you see, it'll just support his prehistoric attitude. He'll think you don't trust me to be alone with another man."

There was a not-exactly-restful silence.

"Brad. You do trust me, don't you?"

After our explosive near-breakup two months ago, this was treacherous ground. Practically a minefield.

Finally Lensky sighed. "You I trust absolutely, Thalia. Him? Not so much."

"In the first place, it's not going to be an issue, because he may be prejudiced but he's not actively stupid. In the second place, even if he did manage to misunderstand the situation, I could deal with him without help."

I could feel the tension in Lensky's body, knew that he still wasn't happy. So I started something that would take his mind off Prakash Bhatia. After a few minutes he joined the program, and shortly thereafter I too forgot completely about the snotty intern.

It would have been about that time on Wednesday night that Annelise pushed her luck just a little bit too far. Up to then the evening had seemed to be a glorious success. Shani Chayyaputra walked into the bar alone, Ben signaled her, she gave Chayyaputra a smouldering look, he bought her a drink and sent out his own signals. "The only problem was," she said, "he was sending so many messages aimed at attracting me that he wasn't telling me anything useful. It was just a constant stream of the usual BS."

"The usual?"

"You know. 'Blah blah blah I'm important, blah blah blah I have an expensive car, blah blah blah I'm rich, blah blah blah want to come for a midnight sail, sweetie?' The kind of trash men always talk in bars."

That may have been what inspired her to take it up a notch, venturing into territory she'd promised Ben she would avoid. She giggled, put her hand on his arm, laughed at his jokes, looked up at him through her lashes - a neat trick, that, seeing she was several inches taller than he was - and generally acted the part of the blonde bimbo who was very receptive to all his suggestions - but at a price. And it wasn't one that could be measured in dollars.

"I told him that I'd simply love to go sailing with him but it had to look perfectly respectable because my father was so worried about letting me live in Austin that I just knew he was having me watched, and if he got a report that I'd done anything like going on a boat alone, at night, with a man, he'd cut off my allowance and make me come back home to Beeville and I'd just die if I had to spend any more time in that boring little town, but maybe tomorrow night we could, you know, double date with my roomie if he knew anybody for her, and I told him she was five feet eleven and blonde and she liked other blonds, so if he knew somebody who was taller than her and kind of fair complected that would be just perfect. And then we could all go on his boat together and that would be perfectly all right but we didn't have to stay together after we got out on the lake and I sure hoped his boat was big enough that we could have some privacy, you know what I mean?"

"And he bought that?"

"Sure seemed like he did, he was practically drooling down the front of my dress by then."

"He was," Ben corroborated when they were filling me in afterwards. "I was beginning to wonder if I'd have to peel him off her by force."

"Silly, I've been dealing with men like him since I wore my hair in two pigtails down my back."

"And I bet you were adorable in pigtails. But if I'd been close enough to hear," he glowered, "I'd have stopped you trying to set up Balan that way, and maybe none of this would have happened."

"You made yourself conspicuous enough as it was."

"Me? I didn't do anything!"

"Except glare at us so much that even he noticed you! He said, 'I don't want to alarm you, but there's a shifty-looking fellow over in the corner who's been staring at you all evening. If that's who your father has watching you, I could neutralize him tonight.' And of course I didn't want him to do anything to you, so I said, 'No, that's just my ex. He's not dangerous, but he tends to show up in places where I'm having a good time and stare at me like that. Don't pay him any attention, he hates being ignored.' But I think he must have had you followed."

"He might have tried," Ben said. "There were some grackles overhead when I left the bar, but I didn't think about that at the time. Anyway, as soon as I got into a nice patch of shadow, I teleported back to our place. He must have had *you* followed, Annelise."

"Wait a minute!" I interrupted. "Grackles? Is Chayyaputra really Raven Crowson - the Master of Ravens? Did you recognize him?" That man had nearly killed some of us last May. And then in October, using the name Jay Corbin, he'd tried to engineer the destruction of the Center by replacing Dr. Verrick with one of his stooges.

"If I had recognized him," said Ben, "I'd have been a lot more worried about the damn grackles. As I should have been…. He *could* have been Crowson, but it wasn't obvious. Not with his hair slicked back in that creepy style, and his skin being a few shades darker…" He shook his head. "Now I can see it, yes. But not at the time."

"Annelise?"

She shook her head. "I never really got a good look at Crowson. He was behind me that one time, you know? With a gun! I remember how his hands felt, and the way he smelled… Creepo-puta was using some gross lilac-scented hair gel that pretty much covered up anything else. And even if he did have power over the grackles, I can't think why he would have had them follow me."

"I can," Ben said grimly. "He had no intention of waiting until the next night to enjoy some 'privacy' with you, Annelise. I don't like to think what might have happened if we hadn't just moved in together."

"I could have handled him," Annelise said.

"A *black magician*, Annelise? And you have no paranormal powers at all!"

"When it came down to it," Annelise said, "I *did* handle him. Remember?"

"A fluke. You got lucky. And it's *not* going to happen again."

She gave him a disgusted look. "Of course not. He's on to us now."

"Guys. Can you stop bickering and tell us what happened next?"


What happened next was that as soon as Annelise got home and greeted Ben, their apartment was invaded by a whirling, chattering cloud of grackles that disappeared to reveal a furious Shani Chayyaputra. "Cheating whore! What is your real game!" he shouted, raising his hand to slap Annelise. Ben got between them, Chayyaputra shouted again and the grackles came back all around them, cackling and clawing. Ben reached for Annelise and caught her arm as the world tilted sideways and whirled around them. There was a stifling darkness, moving and full of black feathers; then they fell out of the cloud of birds into a small room with a stone floor and walls.

Annelise was shrieking, "Let me go!" Chayyaputra had hold of her other arm. He aimed a sideways kick at Ben and made him stagger; then the birds swooped down again between him and Annelise and he kicked Ben again, this time in the head, and knocked him out.

"What did you *do* to Ben?" Annelise screamed.

"Not nearly as much as I plan to do with you," Chayyaputra snarled. "You are in *my* land now. First I'll show you what we do with teasing whores, then maybe I'll let you buy his life by being very, very nice to me." He grabbed the front of her dress and ripped downwards.

# 9. Bollywood freestyle

Thursday was a slow day at the Center. Ben didn't even show up in the morning, and Ingrid was closeted with Colton, working on path-connected spaces and flight. I might as well have scheduled Prakash's little educational session for ten in the morning, except that he wasn't there either; presumably hiding out in the math department again. Fine by me; I was tired of the man and perfectly happy to spend a quiet morning refining my control of playing cards. My fellow reseachers had pointed out that I was a bad liar so many times that I had decided I needed an edge before we got into another poker game. Serve them right if they were so hung up on flashy stuff like flying that they never learned how to select the right cards out of a deck.

By noon, though, the quiet was beginning to worry me. Annelise hadn't stocked the doughnut tray that morning, and in between hunger pangs I called her cell phone, just to make sure she and Ben were all right.

Voice mail.

Ben's phone? More voice mail.

I left slightly testy messages for both of them and invited Lensky to take me to lunch at some place that actually had tables and forks and people bringing food to you.

We were just back from that excursion when the peace of the third floor was shattered by a thump like Colton Edwards trying and failing to fly. Only for once, it wasn't Colton sprawling on the floor; it was Ben, on the public side of the office, looking rather the worse for wear. Atop him was Annelise, who seemed to be wrapped in several yards of bright pink and green fabric with bells on the hem.

Lensky came charging out of his office. "*What happened to you?*"

Ben looked up at Lensky and put an arm around Annelise's waist. "I can explain everything."

"I doubt that! But you may as well try."

He looked at me. "Ah, does Lensky know about, ah…"

"He'll have to now," I said with resignation. I couldn't meet Lensky's eyes. "But you weren't going to do that again after the briefing yesterday. You told me you weren't!"

"Do *what?*" Lensky demanded, and without waiting for an answer, "Exactly what have you maniacs been up to now? Jesus wept! It's like trying to work with a pack of insane toddlers. Insane *flying* toddlers, God have mercy on me!" He turned his back on all three of us. "My office. *Now.*"

He didn't have enough chairs. Ben scavenged in Jimmy's office and brought in a couple more chairs for himself and Annelise, moving slowly and carefully as though Lensky were an unexploded bomb. That was probably appropriate, actually. I was just glad that he had more targets than me this time.

"Brad," I said while Ben was micro-positioning chairs, "you know that thing where you promise not to get mad and pound the floor with your shoe? Well, this would be an *excellent* time to do that."

"What, hit someone with my shoe? Don't tempt me!"

"No, promise not to lose your temper. I think this is going to be somewhat complicated to explain, and we won't be able to get it straight if everybody's yelling."

"Too late," Lensky said. "But don't worry about that. *I'm* the only person who's going to be shouting. The three of you are going to be explaining how a direct request to stay far away from Sandru Balan led to Ben falling out of mid-air and Annelise dressed like an exotic dancer and Thalia looking like the dictionary definition of *guilty*."

"Exotic dancers don't wear *nearly* this much fabric," Annelise said.

Lensky sank down on his own chair, rested his elbows on the desk and his face in his hands. "Tell me that you can make more sense than that, Thalia."

"We just wanted to help," I started. "And this began *before* you briefed us on Sandru Balan."

"But *after* I told you on no account to get mixed up with verifying Blondie's – Balan's – identity, right?"

"Ye-es, but we *weren't* going after Balan. We just thought it might be useful to find out a little more about the man he was meeting with."

"Shani Creepo-puta," Annelise said.

"Chayyaputra."

"I like my version better."

"Oh, and Jimmy helped us," I said, "so you might want to invite him in here to be yelled at too."

Lensky glowered. "Jimmy is relatively sane. I bet he didn't do anything worse than providing information for you three to misuse."

"Well, anyway…" I took him through the initial plan for Annelise to chat with Chayyaputra while his face got darker and darker and the vein on his left temple started dancing up and down.

"And that was it," I concluded. "Two evenings, and she never saw Chayyaputra, and after your briefing yesterday morning we agreed to shut the whole thing down. *Didn't we, Ben?*"

Ben danced around the topic evasively until forced to admit that all right, after I'd left Annelise had persuaded him to give it just one more night. Strangely, this made Lensky chuckle.

"Now you know how I feel, Thalia, when I think you've promised not to do something and you weasel-word your way out of it. Okay, Ben, so what happened next?"

"Annelise was wonderful," Ben said warmly. "She saved us!"

Annelise shook her head. "I had no idea that course Daddy made me take would really work. I never had to do it for real before."

"Do what?" I asked.

"Krav Maga," Ben said. "With an ex-Mossad instructor."

When Chayyaputra ripped her dress off Annelise screamed again, but this time she threw herself forward while she screamed, her free hand held out in front of her. Her palm hit Chayyaputra in the nose and his head snapped back. She followed up by stamping her heel onto his foot, pushing down from her hips. A kick to the side of his knee had him on the floor. She finished with another stamp, this time on his tenderest parts. "Oh, my," she said, looking down at his writhing form, "it actually worked!"

Ben was on his hands and knees, his head swaying. Annelise grabbed his arm and hauled him to his feet while Chayyaputra was still curled up and moaning. "We have to run!"

"Where?"

"Anywhere!" There was only one opening in the stone walls surrounding them. Annelise dragged Ben through it, paused a moment to evaluate her options, and took off running to where the crowd around the building was thickest. "Sorry, excuse me, we need to get through here," she babbled while wriggling between staring and pointing people. A flimsy wooden shack was in front of them; she and Ben ducked inside and found themselves half smothered in brilliant fabric.

"Wait a minute," she gasped.

"What for?"

She gestured at herself. Most of her dress had been left dangling from Chayyaputra's hand. "I'm too conspicuous like this." She rummaged through lengths of fabric and found one that she could tie around her waist as a sort of skirt. A second length went over her chest, covering most of the spectacular scenery revealed by her black lace bra.

"Late again!" a little man screeched at the door to the hut. "You are being the American dancer, isn't it? *Jaldee karo*, cannot wait all day! Musicians are expensive!" He turned and called over his shoulder, "*Jaldee* girls!"

A bevy of pretty, dark-haired girls dressed in full skirts and scanty tops came running in, surrounding Annelise and drawing her back outside with them. "Wait," she gasped. "I don't – I'm not – "

One of the girls giggled and chattered at her, with hand gestures. "No time to rehearse," another one translated, "just do like us and follow the music."

Annelise felt like a giantess. A *clumsy* giantess. She was a head taller than any of the dancers and she had no idea what to make of their whirling steps and stylized hand movements. But there was a drum pounding out a heavy rhythm to accompany the flutes and trumpets. She sidled along the line, moving her hips in time to the music and smiling as if she had some clue what she was doing. The other dancers spun away from her, picked up vividly colored ribbons and threw them towards her; bright streams of color flashed over her head and clung to her shoulders. She pushed the entangling ribbons out of her face and tossed her hair. The dancing girls cheered and imitated her movements, shaking out their long dark hair.

That was when she decided to take control of the situation. Whatever it was. She shoved a hip out and posed; the other dancers copied her. She waved her hands over her head, threw her hair back, took two kick steps, and pretended she was dancing freestyle – very free - at the Broken Spoke. The music went on and on and finally rose to a crescendo, then stopped.

"Beautiful, beautiful!" exclaimed the little man who had upbraided her in the shack. "Verree ori-ginal, isn't it? You are dancing for Bharat Studios only, no?"

"Yes," Annelise said. "I mean no. I mean – I need to go now." She pushed her way past dancers and musicians and found Ben sitting in the middle of the costume shed, holding his head.

"After that it was simple," she said. "They were filming some kind of movie, I think, in front of this kind of temple-looking building where that bastard took us. But it was in the middle of a town."

"Simple!" Ben repeated. "No, it wasn't. But Annelise was *wonderful*. She found out where we were and then she figured out how to get us back here."

"You didn't just teleport back?"

"I couldn't get any sense of where Austin was," he told me. "I thought it was because he'd kicked me in the head, but maybe it was just too far away."

"*Much* too far," Annelise said firmly. "We were in a suburb of Mumbai, outside some shrine where they were filming a movie."

"How did you figure that out?"

"Oh, this nice geek at the internet café told me. Then I got on the internet and IM'd Daddy – "

"You had money? Indian money?"

Annelise grinned at me. "Lia, one of these days I've really got to teach you and Ingrid how the world works. A pretty girl should *never* buy her own drinks. I really hated using your money at the Driskill, but I couldn't risk being involved with somebody else in case Chayyaputra suddenly showed up. Anyway, the same principle goes for things like fifteen minutes of Internet time. It makes men happy to give us these little things, why deprive them of the pleasure? And it was much too risky to let Ben even think about teleporting all that way. It might have killed him! I asked Daddy to send one of the jets for us. I was a teensy bit worried about waiting around there in case the creep got over clutching his gonads and came after us again, but it happened that one of Daddy's friends had a jet at Kalina – that's the corporate jet terminal in Mumbai – and he sent a car and driver for us and flew us right back to Austin."

"*One* of the jets…" It sounded like something right out of one of Annelise's wilder flights of fantasy, but she sounded completely matter-of-fact about the whole thing. I tried to wrap my head around the concept that "Daddy" was an order of magnitude richer than I'd imagined.

Anybody who could snap his fingers and have his daughter picked out of a Mumbai suburb and flown back to America probably had ways of getting around Customs and Immigration too. I decided I didn't even want to know about that.

"Well, it was thoughtful of you to come straight back here from the airport. We were getting worried about you two."

Annelise blushed. "Well… not that thoughtful. Actually I wanted to borrow Mr. M. If Creepo-puta busted into our apartment once he might do it again, and…"

Mr. M. indicated his willingness to guard the apartment while Annelise and Ben recovered. He slipped out of my belt and rode off around Annelise's shoulders, resting his little turtle head right over the black lace that peeped out above her wrap.

"*I intend to deal with them individually.*"

"*Fine. Start with the girl Annelise and her boyfriend. I owe them a little extra attention.*"

*"You will allow me to select my own targets."*

*"Within reason."*

*"Very well, let us leave it to chance. Let Lamashtu watch their office, and let her tell me whenever one of the mages is alone. I need to take them when the other mages cannot help them… one or two at a time, as I said… let their fear build."*

# 10. Intoxicated by your touch

I hadn't seen Prakash all day, so I texted him to learn if he was still up for an unofficial work session this evening. While waiting for an answer, I went over to the Student Union and grabbed a hamburger. Teleporting around the university was no longer much of a strain for me, but it was only sensible to make sure I didn't start the evening hungry.

I was debating being extra-sensible with a piece of cherry pie when he texted that he would be there in ten. OK, no pie. If we actually did enough work tonight for me to need a refill, I'd just have to raid Lensky's refrigerator. I stepped out of the Union to teleport back but there were still too many people around for privacy, so I had to walk the short distance back to the office. I even climbed the stairs; there weren't any witnesses inside Allandale House, but I *had* promised Lensky I wouldn't teleport to work until the matter of Balan was settled.

Prakash was waiting for me when I went through the wall. Actually sitting in my office, behind my desk, looking through one of my math books! His jacket was slung over the back of my chair. OK, he'd found a *fourth* way to be annoying: invading my personal space.

He looked up and gave me what I had to admit was a rather dazzling smile. "Thalia! I was afraid you had decided not to come."

"*I* texted *you*," I pointed out. "Are you ready to start?"

He pushed my chair back and came around my desk. "Never more ready," he purred, and tried to put an arm around me. I saw it coming and teleported two feet back before he touched me.

"To start *work*," I said. "That's all."

"It is not work to be alone with a beautiful girl." He moved in again, this time with both arms out, and I teleported to behind my desk. He looked confused. "Why you are running away? You were wishing me here to meet you, isn't it?"

Damn Lensky! He'd been absolutely right. And Prakash had now come up with a *fifth* way to be annoying. "I asked you to meet me here so we could both *concentrate*," I said. "Now it's your choice. Keep chasing me around the desk, and I'll be out of here before you know it. Settle down to work on the Brouwer Fixed-Point Theorem, and I'm here to help you. Which will it be?"

He *almost* pouted. It wasn't a good look on a man in his late twenties, no matter how handsome. "I do not understand women."

"Clearly. I hope you're better with topology."

He heaved a weary sigh and pulled up a chair for himself. "Any continuous function sending a compact convex set onto itself contains at least one fixed point," he rattled off. "This is very basic theorem, Thalia. I understand it already, probably better than you. If that is level on which you are working, you cannot teach me anything new."

"Stick around a few minutes. Do me a favor: visualize an example of that theorem in your math space. Think – oh, think about two planes. Crumple up the top one and let it touch the bottom one at just one point."

He shrugged, but his eyes drifted up and to the right and he didn't, for once, say anything.

"Now replace the bottom plane with an image of where you are right now, and the top with an image of – oh, say, your own office – and let yourself be the point in common."

He blinked hard, but nothing else happened.

"That should have moved you from here to your office." And what a blessing that would be. "Look, it works like this." I blinked and teleported to the hall just outside my office door.

He turned in his chair and clapped his hands. "Very cool trick, Thalia. Do you have the rest of the floor set up like this? Holographic projections? Mirrors?"

I stepped forward, put my hand on his shoulder, and teleported both of us into Ingrid's office.

"I have to give you credit, you must have spent long time preparing this. You did not have to work so hard to spend time with me, Thalia. I am happy to meet you here without any magic tricks."

"What would it take to convince you that I really am teleporting us?"

"Nothing, because I know that it is not possible. You are only playing hard to get, and it is a waste of time since you were already arranging to be alone with me. We both know what is the score, isn't it?"

"We do *not*." I was beginning to suspect he was using the pretense of flirtation as just another way to avoid the mathematical reality before him. "Look, if you think I'm just doing some kind of sleight-of-hand and it's all done with previously set up mirrors and projectors, how about we do it somewhere else? Let's go outdoors. Walk to a place of your choosing – as long as it's out of sight of passers-by – and I will teleport both of us to a *second* place of your choosing. I can't possibly have prepared the entire city for 'smoke and mirrors' effects, no?"

Dammit, now I was starting to talk like him.

"That is sweet. Oh yes, Thalia, I will like to be alone with you in a dark place, but outside is too cold, no? Let us stay here and be comfortable."

"Believe me, your virtue is perfectly safe with me. Your *life*, on the other hand…"

"Oooh, I am so afraid!"

"You should be," I said between gritted teeth. I grabbed his elbow and jumped both of us, fast and hard, to a place between a cluster of shrubs and the front door of Allandale House. "Since you wouldn't pick a starting point, I have. Now where shall we go?"

Prakash gasped. "How you are doing that?"

"I *told* you. Brouwer Fixed-Point Theorem."

"Nonsense."

"How do *you* think we got here?"

"Obviously we came down the stairs. I must have been too intoxicated by your touch to resist you. But Thalia, it is *cold*. Can we not go back inside now?"

It was a bit chilly, even for me, but I was determined to make my point. "First pick a place for us to teleport to. I can take us any place that I've seen before. That would include most of the Drag north of MLK, the West Mall, the South Mall... it just has to be some place without a whole lot of people around."

"After we do this, we can go back indoors?"

"Sure."

Prakash gave his humoring-the-idiot-female sigh again. "Very well. I choose... that miniature Albert Memorial place."

"Littlefield Fountain?"

"Yes. *Now* let us go inside. I am freezing!"

"Good choice. It's unmistakable and unforgettable. Which side of the fountain? I presume, given how much you're whining about a chilly night, you would rather I didn't take you right into the middle of the water."

"Does it matter?"

"When two people are teleporting together, it's a good idea to make sure they're both on the same page."

Another elaborate sigh. "All right. The east side, by the statue of the naked man in the tin hat. But I am not going anywhere without my jacket."

"Whine, whine, whine. OK, I'll *get* our jackets."

A quick round trip to and from the office should have taken essentially no time at all, but I was held up by looking in the wrong place for Prakash's jacket; I'd forgotten that he'd hung it over my desk chair while he was trying to take over my personal space. I had a sweatshirt hanging off a hook in my office, emergency supply for the days when a blue norther dropped the temperature twenty degrees in twenty minutes, and I took a moment to tug it over my head. It wasn't all that cold, but I was beginning to feel that it would be wise to wear multiple layers of clothing around Prakash the Octopus.

He was standing with his shoulders hunched and his arms wrapped around himself when I got back, and he complained about how long I'd taken, but he was still there. I thought that maybe one tiny part of him actually wanted to be convinced.

As soon as he put his jacket on I took his elbow again and put my free hand into my pocket. The stars fizzed and danced against my palm. "Ok, it will help if you can hold those images in your head, the Brouwer Fixed-Point Theorem and the east side of Littlefield Fountain." I didn't feel quite as much drag this time as I had when I whisked us outside; perhaps he was helping a bit. Still, having him along slowed me so that even with the power of the stars helping, I had just time to blink at the colors and shapes and exhilarating movement of sliding through the in-between.

We came through right beside the statue, and the first thing I registered was a cloud of grackles forming a column of black feathers beside Prakash.

"Oh, shit!"

"What's wrong?"

"Grackles."

That was as far as I got before Sandru Balan stepped out of the cloud of grackles. I tried to jump both Prakash and me backwards and raise a shield around us, but I wasn't quick enough. Balan wound up with an arm around Prakash's throat; I wound up two steps away inside a shield that was not going to do Prakash any good at all.

# 11. Liar, liar…

The explosion of the gun was deafening, but my shield held up beautifully. The bullet's energy made me take a couple of steps back, that was all, when it bounced off my shield and vanished into darkness.

"No magic tricks!" Balan said. To Prakash, not to me. "If I suddenly find myself somewhere else the first thing I'll do is shoot *you*. And I'll do the same if your little friend there suddenly disappears." Now he looked at me. "If you want him to live, you'll do exactly as I tell you. You can begin by dropping your protective wall."

I stuck my hands in my pockets. "What makes you think I have some kind of protection? You missed, that's all."

In answer, Balan moved the barrel of his gun, fired at me again and swung it back to Prakash's head. This bullet, like its predecessor, bounced harmlessly off my shield. A faint clang suggested that the ricochet had carried it into one of the bronze sculptures of the fountain this time.

"That's noisy," I observed. "Do it a few more times and I wonder how much of a crowd you'll draw?" Not much, on a cold Thursday night far away from any student residences, but maybe he didn't know that.

"Drop the wall or I kill this one!" he repeated angrily.

I eased my closed fists out of my pockets. *Riemann surfaces.* The picture was bright inside my head, but I held it still so as not to start anything too soon. "You won't shoot him. If you do, you have no other leverage against me."

"Thalia, *run*!" Prakash burst out. "Don't mind me, save yourself!"

He must not have grasped what Balan had, that I was quite safe as long as I maintained the shield.

"Oh, hell, no," I told him. "And don't interrupt me again." It was tricky, holding the image of the covered sphere that shielded me while I simultaneously built Ben's Riemann surface in another part of my math space. Fortunately I didn't have to juggle the visualizations for long. I just wanted to be sure I was completely ready to implement Riemann before I dropped my shield to do so.

"I don't have to kill him," Blondie said. "I think it will suffice if I shatter his elbow. That should impress upon you the importance of cooperating before I have to destroy another joint."

The pistol moved. So did I, opening my closed hands and releasing a brilliant cloud of stars that covered Balan's face. At the same time I mentally moved my chosen points on the Riemann surface to converge on one point a couple of feet in front of me.

His pants burst into flames. He dropped the pistol and Prakash to slap at the flames. I grabbed Prakash, replaced the fire algorithm with the *Brouwer* image and brought us back to the top floor of Allandale House. It was somewhat more taxing than the journey out, because I had carelessly thrown all my stars at Balan's face and had none left to feed into the visualization. I had to make this jump the old-fashioned way, on nothing more than my personal power, and Prakash weighed me down. The jump was long and slow and painful. I felt as if a piece of my soul was being pulled out while Prakash and I traversed arcs and spiraled down in dimensions that shouldn't exist.

Then, just as I was losing momentum at a sharp vertex, I felt some other power pushing me forward. Prakash became light as a feather. Another heartbeat's worth of moving lights and we hit the floor in Allandale House.

I mean that literally. Teleporting someone else with you makes for a tricky landing; unless you started off with both of you standing and balanced, you tended to fall out of the in-between. Somehow topologists in pairs never are that balanced.

We scrambled to our feet and stared at each other. For the first time

Prakash was actually looking into my eyes instead of over my head. "It's real," he breathed.

"You felt it? The in-between?"

His hands were shaking. "I – I *used* it! The Brouwer Fixed-Point Theorem. It works – it really works."

A first visualization, in the middle of a frightening escape, with no pre-planning! Dr. Verrick's intuition had been right; once he allowed himself to believe that what we did was real, Prakash had the potential to be a superb research fellow.

All that flickered through my mind for examination later. Right now I too was shaking. Zipping through the in-between has interesting side effects, such as raising your heart beat and making you dizzy. It also affects the libido.

So, I discovered, does being shot at and missed. Just as Lensky always claimed.

The palm of my open hand prickled; the stars were returning. Prakash stared at the cloud of flashing blue-white pinpoints funneling themselves into my hand

"You saved my life," Prakash said. "I have never met a woman like you. There *is* no other woman like you."

"Actually, Ingrid is almost as good with teleportation…"

He grabbed me around the waist and bent me backwards for a prolonged kiss. He was much stronger than I was, but his manhandling hardly encouraged me to direct my heightened libido towards him. I stood perfectly still and waited for the idiot to finish.

Then, when it began to seem he was never going to let go, I contemplated using Riemann surfaces for a second time tonight. He released me just in time to save his beautifully tailored pants from igniting.

"If you're *quite* through?" I said, backing away.

He looked puzzled. "How you can be so cold? After what we have been through together? It is Fate. Our lives are forever linked."

I laughed outright. "Oh, get over yourself. I've been through worse. With better men." With one *much* better man, to be specific. "Go home, eat something, get some sleep."

"At least let me drive you home. It is cold outside. You should not walk."

It might take him a little while to wrap his head around our special abilities. "I don't have to, remember? Now *go home*. Tomorrow we start serious work." I turned sideways and vanished.

*"After this fiasco, I begin to doubt your usefulness."*

Balan began to think about ways to kill Chayyaputra. Slowly. No one *lectured Sandru Balan!*

*"You have every advantage. My servants spy for you and transport you. And yet you cannot even kill two unarmed people!"*

Chayyaputra seemed angrier than this one incident justified. Maybe something else was bothering him.

*"They have something else, something you did not tell me about! The girl put an invisible wall between us."*

*"Ah. I cannot give you the power to break down that wall, but I can give you the ability to raise a wall of your own. Not that you will need it... but here."*

An iridescent, blue-black feather appeared in Chayyaputra's hand. Scowling, Balan took it and added it to the two feathers he already held.

*"Try not to lose it."*

He would not kill Chayyaputra just yet. Not until he fully understood the man's powers. Besides, after the initial reluctance, he was funding Balan's revenge lavishly – or had been.

*"Initially I did not object to your piecemeal approach. But it seems you are finding it more difficult than you thought to target them. Let us forget half measures."*

*"What did you have in mind?"*

*"Using your primary expertise. A bomb. Can you manage that?"*

Perhaps he would destroy this hotel at the same time. No, destroy the Center, get paid, and then let Chayyaputra learn how unwise it was to annoy Sandru Balan.

*"Of course I can 'manage' it."* You fool, you take your life in your hands when you talk to Sandru Balan like this. I'll have your money first, and then...

*"Then do so. Quickly. I tire of this game."*

Prakash Bhatia found it nearly impossible to go to sleep on that Thursday night. His whole world had been turned upside down. The feats he had dismissed as "smoke and mirrors" were real. And the unimpressive girl he'd considered not worthy of his attention had turned into a heroine – and then she'd left him, flat, without any discussion of their relationship. She'd put herself at risk to save his life! She couldn't be indifferent to him. Women played these games for obscure reasons of their own, but the fact remained. She was an overlooked jewel. *His* jewel; that man Lensky could not properly appreciate her qualities. Only he could do that.

He spent some hours recalling each of their interactions in detail. There was not actually that much to recall; he had been avoiding the Center. But he relived every word, every interchange. He'd been appallingly rude to her – but that was forgivable; unknowing, he'd been fighting an attraction he had not consciously recognized. He would explain that to her in the morning.

By the time he actually slept, Prakash was convinced not only that he loved Thalia, but that he had loved her from the moment they met. Fate had brought them together; what he might have overlooked, Fate had underlined by arranging for her to save his life; if she didn't yet recognize that their lives were bound together, it was only because she had not had time to accept that fact. He would have to save her from her foolish attachment to Lensky.

And he would have to do that while learning a twisted, sideways mathematics that defied reality, while mastering powers he'd never dreamed of possessing.

It was a weighty task, but he had no doubt of his eventual success. Hadn't he graduated with honors first from Indian Institute of Technology and then from Tata Institute? *That* was competition, all those hungry, brilliant minds vying for top marks. This Lensky was nothing; Prakash's only real adversary was Thalia herself, with her misguided loyalty to a man who did not deserve her.

"You shouldn't have stayed up," I said.

I really meant, "I wish to God you hadn't stayed up waiting for me, because I haven't figured out how to minimize what happened." I don't lie to

Lensky unless it's absolutely unavoidable. Tonight's debacle, I reluctantly decided, did not meet that criterion. Besides, Prakash would probably talk tomorrow.

Lensky's lips compressed when I got to the part about teleporting to Littlefield Fountain. I hadn't even mentioned Balan yet!

Well – no help for it. I rushed through the incident at the fountain while emphasizing that I had been in no danger whatsoever. (Not a lie. Just a little shading of the truth. Right?)

"If you're going to yell at me," I said, "I wish you would go on and get it over with." The look on his face suggested that this fight was going to be a doozy.

"I'm not," he said, surprising me. "For once, I'll concede that this wasn't your fault – except for teleporting to a destination where you could be attacked. And I do see how you could have overlooked that in the heat of the moment."

His face was still set in stone.

"You're furious, aren't you?"

"No," he said, surprising me even more. "This expression you see is me *not* saying, 'I told you so.' Speaking of temptation, I take it Bhatia behaved himself?"

"Um – eventually." Discounting that torrid kiss at the end, which Lensky really didn't need to hear about, did he? "Initially," I confessed, "he had the wrong idea, just as you predicted. But I set him straight."

Lensky cracked a smile. "I bet you did. How many fingers is he missing? Oh, and by the way, did he concede that what you do is real?"

"He was shaken up enough to do that. But I wouldn't be surprised if by tomorrow he has decided it was all a bad dream."

"Me too." He wrapped his arms around me. "*My* bad dream. Remember? You were teleporting into danger, and you never came back. You were damned close to not coming back this time. I just hope this was what the dream was about." He took my shoulders and held me away from him, far enough that I could see his face. "You need to be very, very careful. What happened shows that Balan has teamed up with the Master of Ravens – and despite there being no clue in the name this time, it has to be Shani Chayyaputra."

"You did say you'd back the Mathematical Mafia against the Master of Ravens."

"That was before Balan joined up with him. I don't know what the two of them could do together, and I don't want to find out the hard way." He gathered me close again, very gently. "The *worst* way. Thalia... I don't know what I'd do if he hurt you. I don't even want to imagine it."

Then he took me to bed and made love to me very carefully, as if he was afraid I'd break. "You're precious to me," he murmured. "So precious... If you won't take care for yourself, Thalia, will you at least take care of what I love?"

# 12. The Wrath of Thalia

On Friday morning I got a call that temporarily made me forget all about the adventure of the night before. Not that it mattered: I was sure Lensky and Prakash between them would fill everybody in.

"Thalia! Andros didn't come home last night." Mom sounded as if she was crying.

"Maybe he stayed over with a friend and forgot to tell you? I did that a few times and you never got upset." So okay, those times I was with Rick, not with a girlfriend. She didn't need to know that.

"You always told me when you were going to sleep over with a friend!" Actually, I hadn't, but we didn't need to go into that either.

Maybe Andros had a girlfriend. I asked about that.

"Of course not! He's just a baby. Besides, I would know."

Right. Just like she'd known I was spending nights with that rat Rick, my senior year.

If Dad made a habit of belittling Andros and telling him he'd never be a man, I thought Andros might have acquired a girlfriend just to show him.

Mom drew a long shaky breath. "He was here last night. He must have sneaked out when we were asleep. And he took a backpack full of clothes with him."

"You're sure about that?" I'd seen Andros' room. Teenage boy, right? Enough said.

"Thalia! I know every stitch he owns. I bought all his clothes. And I do his laundry."

All right, now I was beginning to share her concern. "Mom. Did he and Dad have another fight last night?"

"What are you talking about? Andros is a good boy. He never raises his voice to his father." She paused. "Yanni might have spoken a little harshly to him. You know he's worried about Andros."

She meant my father Yanni, not my oldest brother Yanni. I'd seen how my father expressed his 'worry.' He'd done the same thing to me, and we'd had explosive fights before I learned to ignore him. Andros never had fought back. Maybe he also had never learned to ignore the constant criticisms as I had. I knew they were getting to him; that had been obvious at Friday night dinner. I began to be worried. Mom could be right, he might have run away. But admitting my concern to her wouldn't help.

"Why don't you try calling his friends? *The ones you know about.* "Even if he's not staying with one of them, they might have some idea how to find him."

After another fifteen minutes of going over the same information, Mom was finally sufficiently reassured to promise she'd do that and to let me go.

When I finally got off the phone, Ingrid was hovering in my office door, looking worried. "Can it wait for a minute? I need to do one more thing." I typed a quick text to Andros... come to think of it, Mom might not even know he had his own phone. I'd set up the account for him last year, since Dad wouldn't do it.

"Where are you? Mom's worried sick and so am I. ANSWER THIS or face the Wrath of Thalia." I sent that off and set my phone to give me a very loud alarm if I received a text message.

"Okay, what's the problem, Ingrid?" And who made me the official fixer of everybody else's problems? Ingrid was the oldest of us – unless you counted Prakash, which I was not quite ready to do.

Of course, I knew the answer. Ingrid was so buttoned-up that nobody felt free to bring personal problems to her.

"Nothing," she said now. "I – is everything all right? You sounded worried."

"I am. But it's nothing you can fix. My idiot little brother seems to have run away from home. Chances are he'll be back tonight, but Mom's hysterical."

"Oh – well…" She stopped and started over, but it felt like a complete change of topic. "I just wanted to ask, how did it go last night?"

In the middle of filling her in my phone beeped, so I wrapped up with, "Tell you the rest later. The important thing is – Balan is working with the Master of Ravens. So watch out!"

I looked at my phone before she was even out of the office. Andros had texted back to say that he was okay but not to tell Mom and Dad where he was.

"How can I, idiot, you didn't even tell *me*!" I counted backwards from twenty and then composed a new text. "I won't tell. WHERE ARE YOU?"

My phone didn't beep for the rest of the morning, so I had plenty of time to warn everybody about Balan and the Master of Ravens and to observe the new, improved Prakash. He was actually in the office we'd made available to him – I wouldn't exactly call it 'his' office yet, he'd hardly used it. But today he was there, and drawing illustrations of the Brouwer Fixed-Point Theorem on the whiteboard. (You can't exactly illustrate the theorem, but you can look at individual examples, sort of. That's what we do when teleporting.)

"Nothing works," he complained when I looked in. "I am studying to the maximum, and it is not working!"

Well, it was sort of my job to help him learn, and maybe it would keep my mind off Andros until he texted back. I studied his drawings.

"Umm, maybe these are too abstract." Hard to be anything else, if you insist on illustrating an existence proof without denoting what it is that exists. I made a quick sketch on the last unused corner of the whiteboard, showing a crumpled sheet of paper touching a flat sheet at just one point. I added arrows labeling the crumpled sheet as "Destination" and the flat one as "Origin," and the point where they touched as "You."

"Why not use flat one as destination?"

"You can do that. But when you need to teleport in a hurry – like last night – it helps if you always use the same image, so you can visualize it instantaneously."

Instead of calling me an idiot who didn't understand reciprocal relationships, he actually nodded and said, "I see. But last night..."

"What were you visualizing then?"

"Nothing... Well, something like you were describing. But if one example works, all should work! Is not logical!" He sounded frustrated. Well, the fact is not much of what we do is all that logical, but I didn't want to upset him even more by explaining that.

"I know. Look, let's practice some real short moves using this example, and when you know exactly how it feels, you could do some research on what visualizations work and if they have anything in common? *Original* research," I added to sweeten the suggestion. "We haven't done much work on the theoretical underpinnings of what we do." Having been too busy getting threatened and shot at and involuntarily teleported and... well. No need to scare him off by a quick recital of Center history. In context, last night hadn't been that unusual.

We worked on triggering the crumpled-paper example by the keyword "Brouwer," and then did some very quick teleports over very short distances – basically limiting the destinations to what he could see from where he was standing, to make it easier.

"Hey, Thalia! You want to go to lunch? And you too, Prakash," Ben added in what was clearly an afterthought.

"No, I wish to stay here only and work on what Thalia has been showing me."

Ben waited until we were outside before raising his eyebrows. "Where is the Blessed Prakash and how did you replace him with this alien?"

"I think last night shook him up a little. Shook him enough to let a tiny bit of light in."

"More than a tiny bit, seems to me. He's actually working. And being polite."

I laughed. "Learning some manners would be a definite improvement. Last night..." I told him about Prakash of the Many Hands. "The amount of hands-on 'work' he was trying to do, I felt like I was with one of those Indian gods with twelve arms! I didn't want to discuss that in the office because, well,

I kind of minimized that problem with Lensky. At the moment he's not mad at me and I'd like to keep it that way."

"Fair enough. Do you want me to join in on tutoring him after lunch? It might not be such a great idea for you to be alone in an office with the guy, if he's that grabby."

"Oh, I think I knocked all that nonsense out of him last night." Except for that Hollywood-style kiss at the end, and the announcement that Fate had bound us together. Oh well, he'd had a night to simmer down and get over that, and this morning he hadn't said or done anything out of line. I figured that particular problem was taken care of.

"Seeing it was you, I'm surprised he has a hand left to grab with, then!"

What was it with Lensky, and now Ben? I am a mild and peaceable person. Despite the rumor Ben keeps trying to start, I do *not* keep a cleaver in my top desk drawer to discourage people from coming in and interrupting me. Not having any chairs for visitors works almost as well.

And Andros had had three hours to text me his location, and he hadn't done it.

When we got back from lunch I was temporarily distracted from that problem. It was clear why Ingrid and Colton had skipped lunch; they had been putting the finishing touches on their project.

When Ben and I got to the third floor, Ingrid was sort of doing the reverse of teleportation and stepping from the floor *into* the air. To be precise, she and Colton were holding hands and swooping through the big central room at the head of the stairs, a good five feet above the floor.

"You made it work? You made it work!"

"Not really," Ingrid called as she swooped by us and did a neat little spiral turn ballasted by Colton's hand. "It turns out to be a completely different topological construct. Nothing at all to do with path-connected spaces! I just thought of it last night."

"And *I*," Colton said, grinning like a fool as he did a sort of breast stroke through the air, "just implemented it."

My eyebrows shot up. "You mean you can do it on your own? Without Ingrid?"

Ingrid folded her arms and shot down to an almost normal position facing me. "We're just starting. But I think Colton is going to be even better at this than *I* will."

Theoretically, any one of us can work any transformation that any other one figures out. But it's true that in practice, we tend to have our specialities. I'd been the first one to use a visualization of the Brouwer Fixed-Point Theorem – well, a lemma of that theorem, to be technical – to teleport, and I could still use it faster and more easily than any of my colleagues. Ben's specialties were shielding and camouflage; Ingrid's was telekinesis. And it appeared that Colton was going to be our aerial acrobat.

Now, as Ingrid shook out the clusters of stars on her fingers and took to the air again, Mr. M decided to serenade us all.

"For you, young Ben," he screeched, and launched into "I Don't Want to Set the World on Fire." Ben's jaw clenched. He was still living down his experiments of last fall, when an attempt to generate light via Riemann surfaces had instead generated fire, automatic sprinklers, and evacuation of the building. He and I had taken apart the relevant mathematics since then, but we'd never been able to get light without fire. That had come in handy for me last night, but in general it got us into more trouble than not. That's why I'm not going to go into the details of how it works; where would we be, I ask you, if the math department were filled with ambitious topologists starting fires at random? I really think Dr. Verrick ought to give us credit for keeping Riemann fire under wraps, next time he accuses us all of being socially irresponsible.

"You had to bring him in today, Annelise?" Ben grumbled.

"He gets bored when he's alone in the apartment."

Ingrid and Colton were still swooping giddily around the room, slowly losing altitude. Mr. M. announced that his next number, "Don't Sit Under the Apple Tree (With Anyone Else but Me)" was going out to Jimmy DiGrazio, whose girlfriend was apparently planning to perch *in* the apple tree with Colton. Mr. M.'s sense of humor tends to be pointed and not particularly kind. We all knew that Jimmy was already insecure about Ingrid's collaboration with Colton.

Fortunately for Jimmy's peace of mind, Mr. M. picked on Colton next. "And for the one unattached member of the Center: "I've got spurs that jingle, jangle, jingle," he crooned. I didn't think Colton was particularly glad he was single, having struck out with Annelise some time ago. He had been eyeing Meadow recently, but like any man with a decent sense of self-preservation, he'd been taking it very slowly.

It was Annelise who finally got our daring young research fellows back down to earth. Their shoes were scraping the floor but they still weren't giving up. She brought the pastry tray out of the break room and waved it at them. "Doughnuts! Chocolate covered, cream filled, raspberry filled! Get them while they're fresh!"

Ingrid and Colton must have burnt up a lot of energy with this flying discovery; they swooped towards the tray and Colton tried to snatch a doughnut. Annelise dodged him. "Sit down and eat like grownups!" She put the tray in the middle of the break room table and the fliers descended on it like grackles sighting a discarded sandwich. I wouldn't have described the subsequent orgy of snatching, cramming and gulping as "eating like grownups," but at least they had their seats in the chairs and their feet under the table. Some days that's the best you can hope for out of our research fellows.

Assuming Mr. M. had been right about practice building up our mental muscles, Ingrid and Colton were going to need some place bigger than the office to build up their flying muscles. So would the rest of us, as soon as they spilled the beans about the mathematics involved – which had better be ASAP. I was not going to be rude or pushy about that. They could finish off the tray of doughnuts first. Then, though, I badly wanted some quality time with Ingrid and a whiteboard. So, to judge from his expression, did Ben.

Colton used up most of our supply of paper towels getting the sugar off his fingers and the chocolate off his face. Ingrid demonstrated a skill considerably more impressive than mere flying: she hogged all three raspberry jelly doughnuts and didn't get a single spot of jelly on her white blouse. "Ah, that was wonderful," she sighed. Slowing down enough to breathe, she started working on a glazed cinnamon spiral.

"Better than teleporting?" Not that I was envious or anything.

"Safer, anyway. Flying, you can see where you're going."

"And when."

Ingrid turned slightly pink. "And when. I think we're all aware of the importance of that part now."

In October, an effort of Ingrid's to push the limits of teleporting had become a demonstration of how to overdo it with star power. Aiming for her home town in West Texas, she and Colton had found themselves in Britfield, all right – the Britfield of 1957. And when they tried to teleport back to now, nothing happened. They had rather a trying time until Jimmy used his talent for research to locate them and his high-powered brain to figure out why the return didn't work. Thanks to that, we now knew a little bit about how time travel worked, but that little was somewhat unnerving. Even Ben hadn't pushed further research into that area.

But I was beginning to suspect that the experience had spooked Ingrid to the point she was afraid to teleport at all. There wasn't any law that you had to teleport whenever possible; on the contrary, Dr. Verrick made it clear to us that we had better not disappear within sight of people who didn't understand the Center's work, or appear out of thin air in front of more such people. So our everyday life didn't involve nearly as much teleporting as you might imagine. We walked down the stairs and to the Student Union, or wherever, to get lunch, and then we walked back. Just like normal people. About all we used teleportation for on a daily basis was to avoid the parking hassle on campus by teleporting between the private side of the office and our apartments, and lots of times we didn't even do that – if, for instance, we expected to need a car during the day.

But Ingrid... I wasn't sure she'd done even that short telecommute since October. And it just didn't make sense that someone who had a way to avoid the nuisance of finding a parking space near campus would go through it *every day*.

We would have to talk about that, but in private, not in front of the entire staff. And any touchy-feely talking was only going to happen *after* she and Colton walked Ben and me through the topology of flight.

"*I'm waiting. Can you do it or not?*"

*Impertinent moron!* "*Can I make a satisfactory bomb out of cigarette lighters and an empty soda can? I too am waiting. By tomorrow night I shall have acquired the materials I need.*" *In fact, he was buying enough for two bombs. First the Center, and then this dolt.*

# 13. A strong desire to duck and cover

The entire Kostis clan was assembled for dinner tonight; Mom must have been on the phone all day. Representing the older generation: Mom, Dad, Uncle Stefanos, and my widowed Aunt Alesia who lives with us off and on. Representing the younger generation: my brothers Yanni and Stevie, Yanni's wife Andrea, Cousin Elias. Representing a strong desire to duck and cover: me.

Hostilities started over the soup (*avgolemono*, in case you're wondering) with Uncle Stefanos opening fire.

"So, Thalia…"

"I pronounce it Thah-lya now."

"What, you know better than your own mother?"

"It's the *Greek* pronunciation, you know." At least I thought it might be. The relevant part to me was that it didn't rhyme with 'failure.' *Why* my parents saddled me with a Greek name and an American pronunciation escaped me, except that it was a part of the general insanity of the family.

"Hah! What do *you* know? Do we ever see you in church?"

"Where," my mother put in, "you might meet a nice Greek Orthodox boy. Now that you've let that Mr. Southingland get away, maybe you'll start coming to St. Elias on Sundays, hmm?"

I jumped up to help her clear away the soup and bring in the main course. At least while I was in the kitchen nobody was yelling at me. But dishing up the food reminded Mom that I'd never learned how to cook and no wonder I couldn't catch a man.

"Oh, leave *la petite* alone," Aunt Alesia laughed her off. "Modern girls do not live in the kitchen, *n'est-ce pas, chérie?*" She patted my hand.

Fifteen years of widowhood have not abraded Aunt Alesia's love for her French husband and have only increased her delusion that French is her first language. Another case of insanity in the family, but a relatively benign one. I was grateful for support, however eccentrically phrased.

Mom ignored the interruption and continued mourning for my lost chances with Ben until Dad interrupted her plaints over the *pastitsio* and beet salad. "Never mind about Thalia." He pronounced it 'Thay-lya,' of course. "All I want to hear from her is where she's hiding that worthless boy."

"If you mean Andros –"

"Do you see anybody else missing? I know you put him up to this! I saw you two whispering in the corner last week! What did you do, tell him he could live with you? Well, he can't! He may be a weakling and a fool, but he's *my son* and he can damn well come back where he belongs!"

"I don't know any more than you do."

Dad glowered at me. "I don't believe you."

I couldn't very well fish my phone out of my pocket and show him the last text I'd sent, given that it started with a promise to Andros not to tell our parents where he was. "He texted me today to say he is safe and all right. I told Mom that. And that is *all* I know."

"Are you telling the truth, girl?" *Thank* you, Uncle Stefanos, for that vote of confidence.

"Who knows?" That was Dad again. "All she learned at that university was to disrespect her parents."

I couldn't see much benefit in continuing to fight. I kept my head down and worked on the *pastitsio* while Dad and Uncle Stefanos enlarged on my many failings, beginning with lack of respect for elders and going on to mention inability to cook, being too plain to attract a man, being too intellectual ditto, and ending with the certainty that whether or not I'd encouraged Andros to run away, the present crisis was my fault anyway for presenting him with such a terrible example.

While I was carrying their plates back to the kitchen and dishing up ice cream, they switched over to Andros. His lack of girlfriends (I'm afraid the boy is going to turn out to be a pervert), avoidance of fights and football (what a wimp) and lack of discipline (Marines? Hah!) were all dragged out and discussed. In detail. Dad only stopped briefly to complain about being fobbed off with ice cream from the grocery store instead of a real Greek dessert.

"I've been too worried about my little boy to cook!" Mom declared tearfully. I suppose the soup and *pastitsio* and beet salad had been assembled by elves.

Dad glared at me while Mom dissolved into tears. "*Now* see what you've done, upsetting your mother? Get out!"

I would have been delighted to walk out into the nearest patch of shrubbery and teleport back to Lensky's, but of course it couldn't be that easy. They thought somebody had to drive me home. Stevie and Cousin Elias both volunteered, and I wound up sandwiched between them in Stevie's pickup truck while they tried to pry Andros's location out of me. As if I knew!

For them, of course, "home" meant the apartment I still nominally shared with Ingrid. And when we got there, worse luck, there was a parking space right outside. Stevie turned off the ignition and announced, "I'm walking you to the door."

"Do that!" I said. "And while you're at it, I suppose you'd like to search the apartment, just to satisfy yourself that Andros isn't hiding in the closet!"

"Good idea," said Stevie, clumping up the stairs with me.

I threw the door open. "Ingrid, are you dressed? My idiot brother wants to search our place for Andros!"

There were a couple of thumps and bumps behind her closed bedroom door and then she came out, flushed and with her hair down, tying the sash on her dark blue robe.

Stevie hadn't seen my roommate with her hair down before, or in a robe that, while technically modest, seriously emphasized her excellent figure. He turned red, stammered, and did no more than glance in her room. I was relieved not to see Jimmy in there; Ingrid might never have forgiven me that embarrassment.

He took longer than necessary to search the rest of the place, though.

Considering how small it was, it shouldn't have taken him more than five minutes to assure himself that we were not concealing a rather large teenage boy.

"Your room is a disgrace, Thalia."

"Thah-lya," I corrected him.

"Don't you ever put anything up?" He skirted a pile of clean laundry and opened the closet. Then he looked under the bed.

"There is hardly room for Andros under there," I pointed out.

"Fair enough." Stevie scrubbed his face with the palm of his hand and ran his fingers through his hair. "You *really* don't know where he is, Thalia?"

"What do you want me to do, swear on the sacred knucklebone of Saint Elias? No. I do not know where Andros is." *And if I did, I wouldn't tell you. Not after hearing Dad going off on him tonight.*

Finally Stevie accepted my word and clumped off to drive Cousin Elias home. Once we heard the pickup start, Ingrid sighed in relief and took off her robe. I was surprised to see that she was fully dressed beneath it. "Ah, Lia? There's one little thing I need to explain."

"What, you've got Jimmy DiGrazio hiding behind your bed? He couldn't come out and say hello to my brother like a normal person?"

"Ah… Not Jimmy, no." She raised her voice. "Andros? You can come out now!"

\*\*\*

I didn't really talk to Andros until the next day; it had been quite late when Ingrid revealed what she'd been concealing from me, and we were all tired and testy. Also, Lensky was expecting me. I figured the rest of the explanations could wait until Saturday. *Early* Saturday.

On Saturday morning, after breakfast at the apartment, Ingrid took off with the explanation that she and Colton had planned to continue working on the flight algorithm over the weekend. It might even have been true. At any rate, she went off in her little Honda – *not* teleporting; that hangup of hers must have been a nuisance – and I made fresh coffee for Andros and me.

"Andy," he corrected me the first time I used his name.

"Andy," I conceded. I was hardly going to argue if the kid wanted a more normal name. Especially since nearly the first thing I told him was to pronounce my name Thah-lya instead of Thay-lya. Not that that was any closer to normal, but at least it didn't sound like "failure."

"So. I know Dad's been giving you a hard time. Was there anything specific that made you decide you couldn't take it any longer, or was it just the cumulative effect?"

Andros – Andy – flushed. "He started in again Thursday night. The usual. I'm a wimp because I never fight anybody, I must be afraid to play football for my school, I'm probably a fag, I'm a disgrace to the family. *You* know. You've heard it all before."

I had, and it was one reason why I ducked out of Friday night dinner whenever possible.

"But Thalia... this time..." He looked down and almost whispered. "Thalia, I wanted to hit him. I almost *did*. That's why I had to get out."

"Oh." That had not been among my reactions to Dad's constant bullying, but then, I was significantly shorter and slighter than he was; it wouldn't have been an option. Andros – *Andy*, dammit – was big for his age, maybe a head taller than our father. And despite Dad's insinuations that he was a wimp and a weakling, I happened to know that he worked out with weights in the school gym on a regular basis. If he'd slugged Dad, our father would probably have gone flying across the room.

"Well, if you ever do hit him," I said after thinking it over, "could you do it on a Friday night, so I can watch?"

"Thalia, it's not funny!"

"No, it isn't. Sorry. I'm kind of a jerk sometimes. So did you leave because you were afraid the temptation to hit him would be too much?"

"Sort of. I figured either way, it would come to the same thing. I mean, what if I did hit him? He'd throw me out, wouldn't he? This way I'm out of the house and I don't have to feel guilty about it."

"No, you can just feel guilty about the fact that Mom's in hysterics and you're planning to throw away your chance of graduating high school."

"That would happen anyway. If he threw me out."

I couldn't argue with that, though I tried. "Andy, your life will be much, much easier if you can stay at home until you graduate. In two years there'll be nothing to stop your enlisting. A year and a half," I corrected myself; his birthday was in June. "Are you *sure* you can't take it for just another eighteen months?"

Andy gulped. "You heard him last week. Thalia, he's getting *worse*. And most of the time I'm the only one there. Since you moved out. Stevie and Yanni don't like coming over much more than you do."

And while I was living at home and working my way through college, I'd been Dad's preferred target, giving Andy some cover. "I do see your point. Still – it's going to be hard, Andy. Where will you live? What kind of a job can you get? If you wait until you can enlist, I think the military will pick up the tab for at least a couple of years of college."

"Thalia, I *can't*. You don't know what it's been like since you moved out. Look, *you* got away. That's all I want – to get away from him. And I thought… maybe you'd let me stay here?"

It probably wouldn't help to point out that I'd taken Dad's criticisms for four long years until I graduated and got a job. If Andros – *Andy* – said he couldn't take it, he couldn't. And I couldn't see sending him home and waiting for the inevitable explosion, even if he would have gone.

"Andy," I said as gently as I could, "it wouldn't work. They'd find out you were here soon enough; you can't keep diving behind Ingrid's bed every time you hear somebody coming up the stairs. And once they find out, you'll be right back where you were. They can probably force you to come home."

"If they do," he said, "I'll just run away again."

"Is there any way I can make it easier for you to last out until you're eighteen?"

He blinked. Rapidly. I looked away so he could swipe a hand over his eyes. "Thalia, if *you* could talk to them? Make him lay off me?"

I'd never been able to do that for myself. I'd just kept my head down and concentrated on getting through from one day to the next.

But maybe – just maybe – I'd be able to do for Andy what I hadn't done for myself.

I had to. He was my kid brother. I'd been what, thirteen when he started school? I'd been the babysitter, the big sister he went to when he had problems at school, the one who listened to him and encouraged him.

The one who'd abandoned him without a second thought, the minute I had a chance to escape.

"I'll try. Tomorrow? Right after church. Maybe he'll be in a better mood then. And can I tell Mom I've seen you and you're okay for now? She really is worried sick, you know."

"She never worried enough to stand up for me," he said with some bitterness.

"She can't, Andy. She really can't." I'd worked my way through that, one painful bit of understanding at a time. If Dad had ever hit us, she might have summoned up the strength to protect us. But bullying? She accepted that as a normal part of life. Her father hadn't been any sweetheart either. She couldn't even let herself see that what Dad was doing was wrong, much less stop him.

"But *you* can," he said with touching, if misplaced, faith.

I guessed I was going to have to.

"Okay. Tomorrow I'll try. But only if you let me tell Mom you're all right." And *that* was going to be a conversation and a half, with me trying to keep them from guessing that he was hiding out at my place after all. In emergency, I might be able to stash him at Lensky's condo. But I'd succeeded in keeping my family from finding out about Lensky for over six months now; I didn't want to give up now. Besides, it wouldn't be any kind of a long-term solution. Although…

"Andy, I've had sort of an idea. But let me try with Dad first, okay? If that doesn't work out, maybe we can find some other solution. Today I've got to go in to work. Will you be all right here by yourself?" I needed to try my crazy idea without his hearing about it.

Of course he'd be all right. He'd brought his Gameboy.

# 14. Elvis meets the Ramones

I spent a chunk of Saturday making sure my alternative for Andros would work, at least short-term. I spent much of the rest of it breaking into a cold sweat at the prospect of negotiating with Dad. I'd always preferred to deal with my family by evasion, dissimulation and denial. Did I really owe it to Andros to put myself through the wringer?

Well yes, I did.

Possibly I owed it to myself as well.

At least, thanks to Colton's nice-guy instincts, I could forget about the problem for a few hours that night. On Friday afternoon, he'd surmised that Prakash was clinging to me because he thought everybody else was still annoyed at him for having been so rude and dismissive before.

"He's not wrong," Ingrid said.

"Come on, Ingrid. You don't want to spend the semester feuding with the guy."

"How do you know what I want?"

"As a favor to *me*, then? I want to be more – more like we were last fall. Almost a family. Being pleasant to one another."

Ingrid sniffed, but she didn't actually turn down Colton's new idea. The boy thought we could invite Prakash out for a Saturday night of live music, dancing, and beer. That would help him feel accepted, and once he felt accepted he would relax and realize that nobody in the Center held a grudge against him.

"We don't?" Ingrid queried.

"You're too kind and generous to keep making the poor schmuck pay for having made a bad start with us," Colton told her.

I don't know where he kept getting this idea that the rest of us were nice people, but he pushed it with enough vigor to shame us into pretending to be what he claimed to see in us. The pretense was a lot easier once he mentioned that Two Tons of Steel was playing at the Broken Spoke the next night. "*I'm going regardless,*" Colton said. "They played Lubbock summer before last..."

I liked them too, as did Jimmy, and even Ingrid allowed that if you were going to go out dancing you might as well have a band that played danceable tunes.

Lensky and Prakash gave us blank looks. "Broken Spoke?" Lensky said. "Country music and line dancing?"

"No. Two Tons of Steel is more.... "I groped for a comparison. "They're kind of like what Buddy Holly would have done if he'd been a punk rocker."

"Who?" That was Prakash.

I tried again. "Elvis meets the Ramones?"

"Oh, *Elvis!*" Prakash said happily. "Hound Dog, isn't it? Heartbreak Hotel? Very good."

"Who are the Ramones?" Lensky said.

"Oh, just come along. You don't have to dance if you don't like it. And there's beer."

I felt slightly guilty about leaving Andy alone with his Gameboy again, but he didn't appear to be suffering; I brought home a sack of cheeseburgers which he wolfed down before getting back to the serious work of breaking past Level 7 of something called DeathVikings.

The Broken Spoke did provide a good setting for mending fences: it was too noisy for conversation, so Prakash couldn't annoy anybody even if he tried. While the opening band played, the Center for Applied Topology, individually and collectively, made a serious dent in the beer supply, occasionally shouting something stupid over the music. Then Two Tons of Steel came on with "Busted," and Jimmy and Ingrid moved out onto the dance floor. Annelise and Ben joined them, and then Meadow started dancing by herself until Colton slipped up beside her and started copying her moves. I tapped my toe to the music until Lensky took the hint. We got in on the end of "Busted" and kept going through "Crazy Heart," which had a stronger rhythm. Lensky started on some swift moves twirling me around the floor. I glanced at Prakash as we whirled by; he had forgotten his beer and was tapping one hand to the music. It really wasn't going to be much of a fence-mending if we all abandoned him. I was about to go talk to him when he moved out onto the dance floor by himself and astonished us all.

The man had some serious dance moves! As "Not that Lucky" started he just about took control of the floor. He put one hand out, steady, while the other one flickered in and out. Bent his knees and swiveled in time to the backbeat, slid across the floor around somebody's girl and back to the center. He reached out and took my hand. "Thalia, dance with me!"

"Tell him to remember I'm carrying," Lensky grumbled as Prakash raised our hands and twirled me under his upraised arm and against his body. I spun out again; the music speeded up, Prakash caught my wrists and the next thing I knew, I was flying through the air.

Lensky's big, firm hands caught me and set me upright again. "What is it with you and men always throwing you into the air at dances?"

That was an exaggeration. There'd been only one other such episode, and like this one, I hadn't instigated it.

Prakash didn't seem to be bothered by having lost his partner. He spun in a dizzying circle with knees and hips and hands all moving to different beats, then caught Annelise's hand and spun her in towards him. He didn't try to throw her in the air, though. A wise decision; she was almost as tall as he was and not exactly sylph-like. Instead he bent her backward and *almost* kissed her. For much too long; Ben was starting to twitch when he let her go again. But that wasn't quite the end of it; he sidestepped towards her and she stepped away, moving her hips like his. They circled halfway around the dance floor before he reached out for Ingrid and spun her to him. The same sequence followed, the prolonged not-quite-kiss and the stylized pursuit, except that Ingrid didn't make much of an attempt at dancing away. Prakash came up behind her, put his hands on her hips and danced her around the floor until she broke away and spun back to Jimmy, flushed and laughing. By this time hardly anybody else was dancing; they were all enjoying the free show.

"Remind me again," Ben grumbled, "exactly whose idea it was to make this guy feel at ease with us?"

"Not mine," said Jimmy. "In retrospect, I'd like to go back to Prakash the Stuffed Shirt."

The band's version of "Diggin' the Boogie," was coming to an end when Prakash spotted Meadow and took her hand. He turned and pulled and nothing happened. "Why you are not dancing with me?"

Meadow stayed planted where she was, a short, solid girl with enough inertia to slow down a train, and the music stopped.

Colton was smirking.

"Where did you learn to dance like that?" Ingrid demanded of Prakash. Now that the band was taking a break, we could hear each other talk.

"Bollywood," he said. "I am great admirer of Bollywood musicals. Some moves I learned from watching Shah Rukh Khan in "Chayya Chayya," you would say, "Shadow Shadow." Classic dance filmed on top of moving train, no stunt men, no fancy editing! Of course Shah Rukh Khan getting too old for that now. But also I study moves of Ranveer Singh in *Befikre*. Many friends say I look like Ranveer Singh, only taller."

"I don't believe he *has* many friends," Jimmy said under his breath.

Colton's fence-mending party seemed to be delivering mixed results.

Even Lensky complained a bit on our way home, though Prakash's demonstration of being an equal-opportunity girl-grabber seemed to have reassured him somewhat. He did say that it served Prakash right when Meadow wouldn't let him spin her around like everybody else.

"Meadow has three inches and fifty pounds on me," I said. "I can't copy her methods of dissuading men."

"Didn't see you doing anything at all to dissuade the guy," Lensky grumbled.

"What did you want me to do, break his nose? He was just in a good mood and wanting to dance with everybody."

"I liked it better when he was in a pissy mood," said Lensky, aligning himself with Ben and Jimmy. "Do you want me to take you to your apartment?"

That seemed like a serious overreaction. "To check on Andros," he clarified.

"No…. He ought to be asleep by now. And if he isn't, I don't want to know. Let's just go on back to your place."

"It's too bad you can't just let him have your room at the apartment," Lensky said, surprising me.

"Why?"

"I rather like knowing that you're going to spend the night with me."

I spent most nights at the condo already, so this too surprised me. It was good to know he didn't feel crowded, but I wondered if he was hinting that I ought to give up the apartment. That made me nervous; I wasn't ready to burn all my bridges yet. We'd only been together a little over six months and I wasn't sure where we were going. Didn't much like thinking about it, either. Everything was good right now; I told myself to enjoy the present moment and not to brood over the future.

I deflected this line of conversation by explaining exactly why Andros couldn't simply move into my room. The whole family knew I had that apartment. I might have been able to get rid of Stevie last night, but I had only succeeded because I really hadn't known Andros was there. Now that I knew differently, it would be almost impossible for me to lie convincingly. And they wouldn't give up. Yanni, Stevie, Cousin Elias would all be dropping by at all hours, hoping to catch sight of Andros.

I managed to keep talking along those lines until Lensky pulled into his covered parking space behind the condo.

"Thalia, he's *your* brother," he said then. "I'm not going to try to tell you what to do. If you think your apartment isn't a good solution for him, you're probably right. In any case, it's nothing to do with me."

If only that were true.

Saying nothing was probably the best way not to be caught lying. Not to mention that I really don't like lying to Lensky. But Dr. Verrick held that if you didn't actually say anything untrue, merely allowed the other person to misunderstand what you did say, you weren't really lying. At the moment I liked that definition.

***

Mom was delighted to see me show up, unannounced, for Sunday lunch. Dad commented unfavorably on my manners: couldn't I have called to let them know I was coming?

Mom put a plate piled high with food in front of me. Dad asked if she thought I couldn't feed myself now that I'd left home.

I swallowed a couple of times and launched into my prepared speech. "I need to talk to you about Andros."

That was as far as I got before Dad's fist landed on the table, rattling all the dishes. He shouted that Andros was no son of his, and the idiot boy needed to get himself back home at once!

Have I mentioned that my father does not have a strong need for intellectual consistency?

His need to be seen as the master of his family, on the other hand, is close to mania.

When she could get a word in edgewise, Mom asked, "Have you seen him? Where is he? Is he all right?"

"Yes, I've seen him. He is all right and he wants to come home." Okay, a slight exaggeration there.

"Nothing stopping him!" Dad yelled. "He can come back whenever he's ready to beg my pardon!"

"Where is he?" Mom implored.

My hands were shaking. Ridiculous! But the prospect of openly defying Dad in his own house was making me dizzy. Part of me was afraid the world would end. The other part was afraid that once I started, all the anger and humiliation I'd been ignoring for years would come pouring out of my mouth and I'd be responsible for a permanent rift in the family.

"I am not going to tell you where he is unless we can come to some agreement about how you treat him." At least my *voice* didn't shake. Yet. And the world didn't end, either.

Yet.

Dad barked that it was none of my damned business how he disciplined his son. He went on to say that it was all my fault Andros had run away, that I'd always been a bad influence on the boy, that he'd known no good would come of letting me go to college, et cetera, et cetera. When he slowed down I repeated what I'd said, a little more forcefully.

"If you talk to me – and shouting insults doesn't count – maybe we can persuade Andros to come home."

"Hah! He'll be back with his tail between his legs soon enough! The boy's a weakling, he can't take care of himself. And *you* aren't going to come between us, Thalia! If you plan to help him, I'll… I'll disown you!"

"Yanni, please!" Mom was weeping. "I've lost a son. Don't make me lose my only daughter too!"

Mom's tears were a large part of why I never defied Dad. Seeing her like this made me feel like somebody was stomping on my own heart. I felt unbearably guilty for hurting her.

Did I have to choose between Andros and my parents? How could he ask me to do this?

I balled my hands into fists to stop them shaking and reminded myself that Mom and Dad were adults. Andros was just a kid, and he didn't have anybody but me in his corner. Me and, maybe, some of my acquaintances.

"Dad! Do you know why Andros left?" I could hear myself getting shrill. The hell with it. There was one person in this room who was responsible for the high decibel level of family conversations, and it damned sure wasn't me. "He ran away because he was afraid that if you kept putting him down and bullying him he would *hit* you! And he didn't want to do that! He wants to love and respect you as if you were actually a good father to him, but you keep tearing him down! What did you expect?"

"I am his father! He owes me love and respect! Haven't I raised him? Now he wants to whine because I'm trying to make a man of him – all right, let him snivel! Let him run and hide! When he gets cold and hungry he'll be back and he'll have learned to mind his manners!"

"Right, because you've given him such a fine example!"

"Thalia," Mom almost sobbed, "what's come over you? How can you talk to your father like that? He loves you, you're breaking his heart and mine too."

My own heart was not doing so great either. I felt like a monster, making Mom cry like that. Oh, I'd gone about this all wrong. There must have been some way to have a quiet, civilized discussion and I'd failed to make that happen. Of course I had. No wonder my name as they pronounced it sounded like "Failure." That's what I was.

I wanted to teleport right out of there before they could see how upset I was. Ever since this started I'd protected them from the knowledge of what I really did. Now – what did it matter if they did see me disappear, what did anything matter? Mom was right, Dad was right, all I did was damage the family. The best thing I could do was to go away and stop making trouble.

*That's not the best you can do for* Andros.

Sometimes I hate having a conscience.

"This isn't about me. Hate me all you want, but think about Andros. Don't you w-want him to come home?" Dammit, now my voice sounded all wobbly. Dad would never listen to me if I showed that I was on the verge of coming unglued.

*What the hell, he doesn't listen to you anyway.*

I cleared my throat and continued. "He has a safe place to stay. And no, it's not with me or with any of my friends. He would rather come home, he *wants* to come home, but he can't unless Dad lays off him. Don't you get it, Dad? He ran away *because* he respects you, because he didn't want to forget himself and hit you. But you need to treat him with respect too."

Dad yelled and cursed and pounded the table for another half hour, but he couldn't get around those facts: Andros didn't have to come home, and he wouldn't come home unless there were some changes. It was entirely possible that they would never see him again.

I came in for a lot more abuse for encouraging a boy to defy his family, setting a bad example, the usual. That wasn't so bad. I had a lot of practice in letting Dad's tirades roll off my back. It was making Mom cry that really tore me up.

We finally agreed that they'd meet Andros at Tino's Restaurant that night – I felt strongly that a public place was necessary to inhibit Dad's ability to throw a conniption fit – and they'd 'talk.' That was as much of a concession as I could get. I hoped it would be enough.

After we agreed on a time for the meeting, I said a quick good-bye and headed out of the house. There was a convenient hedge just around the corner where I could duck out of sight and teleport home.

"Home," in this case, being Lensky's condo.

# 15. The sacred knucklebone of St. Elias

Once there, I called Andros and told him when and where we were going to meet our parents. I also told him that yes, I definitely had a place where he could stay if the meeting didn't work out, and I wasn't going to tell him where right now because it might be better if he *couldn't* tell Dad any more than that he had somewhere to go.

Of course he trusted my promise. I was his big sister. We might have squabbled, growing up, but he knew I was on his side.

Good thing I was telling the truth about having a bolt-hole for him. He would have believed me anyway.

Then I threw my cell phone across the room and very calmly smashed three mismatched saucers and a thrift-store bud vase I'd never liked anyway.

"What did they *do* to you?" Lensky asked when I got a broom and dustpan to clean up the mess. He hadn't stopped me breaking the dishes, which I appreciated.

"Nothing. Just a lot of yelling. I don't know why it got to me this time, Dad was a total pill for the entire four years I was going to college and living at home to save on rent. All that time I never fought back; I just kept my head down and stayed out of the house as much as possible. At least that way I wasn't making things *worse*. Now – oh, I was trying to help Andros, and instead I made Mom cry and I made Dad lose his temper. I'm just no good with people."

"You're pretty good with *me*," Lensky said gently.

"I seem to recall that you've been annoyed with me yourself, once or twice."

"Yes, well, I didn't say you couldn't be infuriating at times. But I do love you. And I suspect your parents do too."

"I'm not so sure about that. Dad obviously despises me. And I don't think Mom will ever forgive me for taking Andros' side. *Andy's*," I corrected myself. "But at least they're going to meet us this evening. In a public place; maybe that'll cut down on the yelling and table pounding."

"Where?"

"Tino's. Naturally since Mom cooks Greek food – well, Greek-American," I corrected, remembering her fondness for dishes involving mini-marshmallows and Jello, "seven days a week, when they do go out to eat, it has to be a Greek restaurant."

"I'll come with you."

"You can't! They don't know about you."

"Thalia, we've been practically living together for six months. They're bound to notice eventually."

"Maybe." I dreaded the day when Lensky would get sucked into the dysfunctional maelstrom of my family. It was one thing for him to accept a girlfriend who could step in and out of thin air. Accepting my insane family might be too much to ask. And I shriveled internally when I thought of him hearing what Dad thought of me. What if he realized that Dad was right, that I wasn't that much and certainly nothing special? "But not now!" Besides, it was looking like I might have to keep my promise to Andros. If the family met Lensky now, they'd have a clue to where I meant to stash Andros until Dad saw reason. I explained that to him without going into my other fears.

"You could have told me that part last night," he said, sounding disappointed.

Well, yes, I could, except that I was in the habit of not telling people things if I didn't have to. I tried to make him see that this was a necessary survival strategy for living in the same town as the rest of my family.

"But was it necessary to leave *me* out of the loop?"

"No. Yes. I don't know. If you didn't know, nobody could blame you."

"I'd still rather know what's going on," he said. But he reluctantly agreed to stay out of it for the time being.

I wasn't nearly so understanding when I got to the apartment and Andros told me that he didn't want me to come to Tino's with him.

"Andy, are you nuts? Dad will eat you alive!"

"If I can't even meet them on my own, how am I ever going to go back? Or were you planning to move back in there to protect me?" He managed a slightly crooked grin. "You can't spend the rest of your life looking after me, Thalia. For one thing, I don't think you'd like it in the Marines."

My kid brother seemed to be growing up fast. I was proud of him – and terrified for him. I called a car to take him to Tino's, waved good-bye with a smile pasted to my face, and went back upstairs to wear a hole in the apartment floor by pacing around the living room. He would be coming back here; I couldn't take refuge at Lensky's place until I knew how the meeting had gone.

I'd seen Andros off at 5:30 and didn't expect to see him back for several hours. All the same, I couldn't bring myself to leave the apartment. I borrowed one of Ingrid's books and tried to lose myself in the intricacies of paracompact spaces. The words of the text floated in front of my eyes while in my head I was seeing an unimpressive strip-mall restaurant with plastic-topped tables. It suddenly seemed important to know whether Tino's tables were bolted to the floor or freestanding. Not that I really thought Dad would go from pounding on the table to throwing it...

It was time to turn the page; I'd read all the words on it. But I hadn't taken in one of them. Studying was *not* going to work.

Oh, well. Ingrid was out somewhere, probably with Jimmy, so the only person I was fooling with a pretense of calm was... me. And I wasn't fooled.

The screen door downstairs slapped against the doorframe and I heard somebody heavy trudging up the stairs. I flew to the door. "Andr – Andy! I didn't expect you back so soon! How did-"

The defeated look on his face stopped me.

"It's no good, Thalia. Dad started shouting the minute he walked in the door. I might as well never have gone. I called Uber after he'd been going for

107

ten minutes. It took another ten for the car to get back to pick me up and he never did slow down while I was waiting. Twenty minutes of yelling was more than enough."

"I should have gone with you."

Andy shook his head. "Sis, I love you and you've done a lot for me, but even you can't work miracles. It's hopeless!" He frowned. "You *did* say you had another idea?"

"Yes, but I wish it hadn't come to this. Listen, Andy, I'm going to tell you some things that I really don't want Mom and Dad to find out about."

"If it's about your ability to disappear," he said, surprising me, "I've known that for *months* and I haven't told anyone."

"What! I thought I'd been discreet around the family."

Andy shrugged. "You don't need to be that careful around Mom and Dad, they never notice anything they don't want to. I followed you a couple of times and saw you duck behind the neighbors' hedge and never come out. Did you go invisible, or were you teleporting to somewhere else? What other cool stuff can you do?"

"Um... I'll tell you some time. This is actually a different type of secret. I'm seeing somebody."

"Mr. Sutherland? I thought he just moved in with somebody else."

I mentally wiped the sweat off my forehead. At least my kid brother didn't know *everything* about me. "No. I was never 'seeing' Ben that way. Mom just wanted to believe we had a thing going, and I let her think that because it discouraged her from trotting out nice Greek Orthodox boys from St. Elias for me. This is somebody Mom and Dad have never heard about, and I want to keep it that way."

"Why? What's wrong with him?"

"Not a thing in the world," I snapped. "Quite the reverse. He's *sane* and I dread to think what effect meeting my family could have on him."

Andy shrugged. "Okay. Is that who I'm going to be staying with?"

"No. His sister-in-law lives here too. Pam has a spare room right now since she broke up with her 'friend' Jerry, so it's just her and Linda – Lensky's niece – in the house. She doesn't know you're underage and a runaway, she just knows you're a young relative of mine who needs to rent a room for a few weeks."

"Lensky," Andy said slowly. "That's kind of a funny name."

Which I hadn't meant to let slip. Ben's right, I am a *terrible* liar. "Polish," I said briefly.

"Oh! Now I remember. He's the spy at your work! That's who you're seeing?"

I flung up my hands. "Yes, not that I meant to tell you that either. You're too damned smart to drop out of school, Andy! Swear not to tell them anything?"

"It doesn't look like I'll have the chance," Andy said ruefully.

"Nevertheless. Swear on the sacred knucklebone of Saint Elias or I won't take you over to Pam's." (I don't actually know whether the church Mom goes to has a relic of its namesake saint; Stevie and I had made up this oath as kids and all four of us observed it as faithfully as if Saint Elias himself were checking on us personally.)

Andy repeated the words solemnly and then destroyed the effect by breaking into a wide grin. "Are you going to *teleport* us to Pam's?"

"Might as well, now that I know you know." Another week with Andy and I would have no secrets at all.

"*Cool.*"

*In the small hours of the morning the grackles formed a cackling, spinning cloud that disappeared as he set foot in the deserted office. He had planned ahead, so he had no need of light to set up the mechanism; pushing a single button would start the deadly countdown until morning, when he hoped the maximum number of people would be gathered there. He would not have to be nearby to trigger anything; once he had left the package, everything would proceed automatically to its fatal conclusion.*

*Finding a place to leave the package was a problem of a different order. How to ensure that it was in a central location, yet would remain undetected? The blank wall to the right of the stairs offered no hiding place, and the private offices opening off the central room were all locked. Very likely Chayyaputra's grackles would be able to transport him into one of those offices, and wouldn't that be a fine surprise for somebody in the morning! But he didn't want to place his package near an outside wall; he'd designed it to have maximum effect in a central location. He switched on the miniature flashlight on his key chain, holding a fold of his shirt over it to keep the light from flashing too brightly, and appraised the room swiftly. A desk — not good, someone might open a drawer. A metal filing cabinet — no, that might contain and diminish the damage.*

*Finally he used the museum putty in his pocket to fasten the package underneath a lightweight table that formed an L-shape with the desk. It wasn't heavy; the putty should be more than adequate to hold it until the timer ticked down.*

*He took one of his three feathers from his pocket and blew on it gently. The grackles returned and surrounded him; time and space tilted around him, until he found himself back in the room he had rented for a short period from someone who had been more than happy to take cash and ask no awkward questions.*

*He slept well.*

# 16. A god of darkness and despair

After settling Andy at Pam's I went back to Lensky's and invited him to distract me from family problems.

"With food? Or something else?"

I realized that I hadn't gotten around to eating all day. Dad had ruined my appetite for Sunday lunch, and this evening I'd been too worried about Andy to get a meal for myself. Anyway there'd hardly been time.

"Food first. Then… use your creativity."

He took that as a challenge. So after making us both sandwiches of prosciutto and fresh mozzarella and hothouse tomatoes, he got extremely creative indeed about distracting me. Outside the condo there was a bleak January night with a hint of snow in the air. Inside was a different world, one that took me away from everything I'd been worried about and challenged me to keep up with Lensky's inventiveness. I couldn't think about anything else while trying to do justice to his attentions. Even had I wanted to.

Monday morning was bright and crisp and the grass outside was white with tiny frost crystals. The clouds were gone and Austin felt remarkably like some place several hundred miles farther north, with nothing between us and Canada but a couple of barbed-wire fences. Had Andy taken his winter coat when he left? I didn't think so.

"He needs a coat," I said unhappily when we were driving to the office. "And he'll be missing school. I *have* to fix this soon."

Lensky's hand covered and warmed both of mine. "Thalia, you can't save the whole world."

"Oh, to hell with the whole world! I just want to take care of my kid brother."

He sighed and carefully refrained from saying that it might not be in my power to do that. I started brooding about what we'd do if Dad remained obstinate – which seemed almost certain. He'd never yet made any concessions to reality and I hadn't seen any hint that this was going to be different. Perhaps I could get a real job, one that paid enough to support Andros and me. Jimmy said his father's company was always happy to hire math majors on the theory that we were smart enough to learn whatever the changing computer world required that week. How much legal trouble could Dad make if Andros stayed with me?

"Lensky?"

"Mm?"

"Isn't there something called an emancipated minor?"

"Planning ahead?"

"Trying to."

"Courts and lawyers can get expensive. Why don't you wait a bit, see if things work out without going to those lengths?"

Good advice, if I'd been able to take it. Unfortunately my default approach to problems is to try and think ahead to the worst possible outcome and figure out how I'll handle that. It required rigid self-discipline to keep myself from doing that about Lensky and me; I didn't have any will power left over to stop myself worrying about Andros.

I was still wrapped up in the problem of Andros when we got to Allandale House. I didn't even complain about the grackles that were clustered all around the building, cawing and screeching and flapping in and out of the trees. Dad was easily worse than any number of grackles, magical or mundane.

Annelise, of all people, brought my attention back to more immediate problems. She and Ben and Mr. M. whisked into the office just after Lensky and I got there; I was still leaning against Lensky's office door and thinking about emancipated minors, hadn't even settled down to my own desk yet. I suspected I wouldn't be able to concentrate on legitimate mathematical problems like refining the flight visualizations, anyway.

"Eeeu," Annelise exclaimed as she lifted Mr. M. off her neck. "What smells in here?"

She poked the toe of one shoe into a white blob on the floor. "This looks exactly like bird poop!"

It did indeed. And there were more splotches, making a wobbly circle on the floor. I'd walked right over it without even noticing.

Mr. M. raised his top twelve inches, spread out the hood Meadow had added to his prosthetic body, and sniffed for himself. "Grackles," he said.

"You can tell the smell of grackle poop from other bird poop?" Lensky inquired.

"I can recognize grackle *feathers*," Mr. M. said. "Look!" He breathed out and a tiny wind raced around the office, picking up downy black feathers and two iridescent pinions and spinning them in a miniature whirlwind in the center of the ring marked out by grackle droppings.

Grackles outside the building were bad enough. I wondered what idiot had left a window open for them on the coldest night of the year.

"There is more," Mr. M. announced. "Something has not left this room."

"Like… there's a grackle hiding?" Hard to see where it could be.

"Something that has the stench of those malodorous birds," he said. He slithered off Annelise's desk and began gliding around the grackle poop in ever-expanding circles, his head raised, sniffing loudly as he went.

"What's up?"

Colton must have teleported directly into the private side, as I would have done if Lensky hadn't been so antsy lately about me teleporting into the office. Hearing Annelise, he'd probably come through the wall in the hope of doughnuts and coffee.

"I do not think it is in your desk," Mr. M. informed Annelise.

"What isn't in her desk?"

I stepped back to where Colton stood. "He thinks the grackles left something nasty here."

"Ah!" Mr M. reared up under the table where Annelise stacked paperwork and emitted a long, loud whistle that swooped up and down the scale. We all covered our ears; even Lensky.

"*What* is that godawful *noise?*"

Mr. M. bent his neck and preened. "It is a reproduction of the air raid sirens from the Blitz. It does get attention, does it not?"

"Sure does, sir," Colton said, respectful as always. "But why? We're not about to get bombed, are we?"

"Possibly," said Mr. M. "Can you identify this device?" He was right under the table now, rearing up and looking at the underside – or at something stuck to the underside? Colton got down on the floor and pushed himself under the table.

"Oh!"

"What is it?"

"I … don't want to shake it," Colton said. "Mr. M.?"

"There is a visible timer," Mr. M. said. "Occam's razor suggests that the timer, rather than sudden motion, will dictate the detonation. However, just in case grackles are not as logical as William of Occam, I recommend handling the thing gently."

I thought that teleporting *out* of the office might be even a better idea. While Colton gingerly pried at whatever he'd seen under the table, I glided back to Lensky and grabbed his arm. If I had to teleport, he was coming with me. And Ben could take Annelise, and where were Ingrid and Meadow and Jimmy? Coming up the stairs right now… and Ingrid was afraid to teleport…

"Evacuate the building?" Lensky said, following the same train of thought.

"No time," Colton said, carefully wriggling out from under the table with his hands upraised to hold something about the size of a laptop computer. I saw bunches of wires, something that looked like a circuit board, a small red light blinking on and off. He sat up and stared at the light. "Thirty seconds… twenty-nine…"

He twisted his body sideways and disappeared, still clutching the mystery package.

"Colton, you idiot!" Meadow shouted, too late.

We all stared at the empty place where Colton had been.

"Was that a *bomb*?" Annelise sat down very suddenly, as if her knees weren't quite steady.

Lensky cleared his throat. "It looked like Balan's work – or what we think his work *would* look like, before the explosion. We've only had post-detonation fragments to study, before."

"It's been more than thirty seconds now," Ben said a minute later.

Nobody had anything to add.

"Any idea where he went?"

"He didn't exactly have time to sign the log book!" Annelise said in a high voice that trembled on the edge of hysteria.

"Who didn't?" Prakash had quietly come up the stairs while we were adjusting to Colton's disappearance. We hadn't given him any stars yet; he probably couldn't teleport into the office unaided.

"Thalia, fill him in," Meadow snapped. She stamped into her office and slammed the door.

Explaining to Prakash what we thought had happened was neither pleasant nor easy. Even though I stuck to what we *knew* – grackle spoor in the central office, hidden device with timer, Colton's disappearance – Prakash was as bright as everybody else, and as capable of drawing conclusions from the fact that Colton hadn't returned.

"I do not understand, though," he said, "how you found this device. Do you search the office every morning?"

"Grackles," I said.

"Grackles?"

"Remember Thursday night? I knew we were in trouble as soon as I saw the grackles. Same thing today. We opened up the office and found grackle poop on the floor and bits of black feathers floating around."

Prakash looked, if anything, even more unhappy than before. "Are grackles always a sign of evil?"

"No, sometimes they're just obnoxious black birds trying to steal your sandwich. But we've had a lot of trouble with them. There's this guy who seems to have power over them, or to draw power from them, or maybe both; we're not sure." I gave him a quick summary of the problems we'd had with the shadowy figure we called the Master of Ravens, ranging from kidnapping and assault to a political attempt to destroy the Center.

"I should have told you," Prakash said after this. "But I did not know this about the birds then."

"What?"

"Thursday night. After you went back to get our jackets? A very large grackle came out of the bushes and flew south. At the time I was only thinking strange to see one alone, but now…"

"A spy? That would explain how the grackles knew we would be at Littlefield Fountain; I'd been wondering about that." I stared at the poker chips stacked on my desk and brooded. "But it doesn't explain why they brought Sandru Balan there. I would have expected Shani Chayyaputra…"

A choking sound made me look up. Prakash looked as rigid as a statue. A dark grey statue. After a moment, just as I was beginning to think about the Heimlich maneuver, he drew a shaky breath. "*Who?*"

"Shani," I repeated, "Chayyaputra. Remember when – oh, no, you weren't in the office Thursday, were you? We got the name from Lensky, somebody who might have been seen with Balan, and Ben and Annelise were trying to find out more when he went full Raven God on them. After he used the grackles to get into their apartment, and then to kidnap them all the way to Mumbai, it's clear that he's the same person as Raven Crowson and Jay Corbin. Even if the name doesn't have anything to do with ravens this time…"

"Oh, but it does," Prakash breathed. "*Shani dev…* Thalia, he *is* a god. Shani, god of dark deeds and despair. Chayyaputra means 'Son of Shadow," and the mother of Shani is Shadow. He is a dark god and his vehicle is a large black bird."

"A minor god?"

"Maybe… not so minor."

"An *Indian* god."

"Yes."

"I was wondering why he transported Ben and Annelise to Mumbai."

"He has a shrine there. In a suburb…"

"And somebody just happened to be filming a Bollywood musical using the shrine as background, which he didn't count on and which gave our people a chance to get away." I liked the evidence that "Shani dev" wasn't a god on the Judeo-Christian model, omniscient and omnipotent. Apparently he could screw up.

Prakash wasn't all that reassured. He hovered around my desk, disbursing little bits of lore about "Shani dev" while recommending that I use extreme care in any matters relating to the god. In fact, he thought I should do nothing even remotely connected with Shani. Not likely! Oh, he had a point. Lensky had a point about Balan, too. But we'd beaten the Master of Ravens twice already, without benefit of Prakash's theological insights. And Lensky's nightmare about my teleporting into danger from Balan had already happened, and nobody'd been hurt.

So far the only person who'd really suffered at the hands of these enemies had been… *Colton*. And it would be poor payment for his sacrifice if the rest of us huddled under the bed and did nothing about the maniacs running free in Austin.

I was thinking about that, and nodding occasionally to Prakash, when there was an almighty thump in one of the offices down the hall.

Last fall that would have been Colton, not flying once again.

I felt miserable at that thought, and then jumped up at the sound of a familiar voice cursing whoever had been moving the furniture. "*Colton?*"

He was sprawled in front of his own desk, looking very much the worse for wear: his hands and face were more or less clean but the skin was scorched and he lacked eyebrows, his shirt was torn and his jeans were unspeakable.

"*What happened?*"

Ben, Ingrid and Prakash were on my heels with variations on the same question. Colton stood awkwardly, wincing when he tried to put weight on his right knee. "The bomb's all right," he said.

"Are you?"

"Yeah, yeah, just let me make a call and I'll tell you all about it." He fished out his cell phone and gave it a rueful look. "Broken. Ben?"

Ben handed Colton his phone and he punched a number. "Janaelle? 'S me. Yes, I'm okay. Back in Austin. Well, I *told* you… *I* can't help it if Bud doesn't believe it. Talk to you later, okay?"

He gave the phone back to Ben. "We got any doughnuts?"

# 17. The best makeout site in Floydada county

We trooped to the break room and I started coffee while Ben blinked out to get pastry for refueling. Lensky, Meadow, Jimmy and Annelise crowded into the room, but the only one who spoke was Meadow.

"What the [obscenity] have you been up to now, Colton, and you better [vulgar expletive] tell me the other guy looks [mild blasphemy] worse!" She grabbed his arms and silenced his mild remonstrance about her language by pulling his head down for a kiss that raised the room temperature by about fifteen degrees and was enthusiastically returned. Well, he'd been teleporting through the in-between, which did things to the libido. Not to mention, from all appearances, being nearly blown up. Which was probably as good as being shot at and missed. I don't know what her excuse was, but the two of them were close to needing a private room.

"Ahem." Ben was back with us, holding a box of doughnuts.

The lovers didn't seem to hear him.

He tried again. "Food? Fuel?"

No response.

"*Chocolate*," he said.

Colton came up for air, wrapped one arm around Meadow and reached out the other for the box of doughnuts. Ben stepped back nimbly. "Sit! Speak!"

Colton complied with the first command, but he pulled Meadow down to sit on his knee. "I thought I might never see you again," he said into her exuberant curls.

"I [expletive] *knew* I wasn't going to see *you* again," Meadow said, with something that in anybody else would have been a sniff. But this was Meadow Melendez, the woman as immovable and unsentimental as a tank, so it must have been something else.

Colton inhaled two chocolate-coated doughnuts while we stared at him, and then drained half the coffeepot. "Good!" he said while tilting his mug up for the last drops.

Nobody had ever used that adjective in connection with Center coffee. Perhaps his adventures had caused brain damage.

"Damn it, Colton, talk!"

He leaned back, tilting his chair perilously on the two back legs. Our furniture wasn't built for that kind of treatment from a big, husky young man. It *definitely* wasn't rated for being tilted under a large young man with a woman as solid as Meadow Melendez on his lap. The chair gave a warning creak and Colton straightened up.

"*Was* it a bomb?" Annelise demanded. Colton's tattered, lightly singed appearance certainly suggested as much. "And why didn't it blow you up?"

"Ported back to the farm," Colton said, making a long arm to snatch a chocolate éclair. "Not the house. Out on the west edge."

The western boundary of Colton's family farm now included the house and outbuildings of a neighboring farm whose owner had been hospitalized for twenty years before he agreed to sell his land to the Edwards family. In those twenty years of neglect the farm buildings, never things of beauty to begin with, had suffered from rotten floors and sagging roofs and infestations of insects and vermin until there was no point in doing anything but tearing them down: something Colton's father had been talking about for nearly ten years without ever getting around to it.

"And you remembered the site well enough to teleport to it?"

Colton gave us a slightly shamefaced grin. "Everybody in Floydada High School knows that patch of buildings. I didn't want them torn down either, when I was in school. Behind the old barn was the best makeout site in the county. 'Course, nobody would be using it for that on a Monday morning. I figured this time of day, there'd be nobody there to get hurt, and a bomb could only improve the old site."

"That was fast thinking," I said with admiration. "Ah – what went wrong?"

Colton looked wounded. "Nothing!"

"Burns," Annelise said.

"Blisters," Meadow added, turning one of Colton's hands palm up.

"Scorch marks," said Lensky.

"No eyebrows," said Ingrid.

"Really?" Colton put up one hand to check. "Ow!"

"So what went wrong?" I demanded again.

"Oh. Well. The bomb went off exactly on time. And it was a beauty! Turned the old barn *and* the hen house *and* the stables into piles of kindling. Even if I did get kind of scorched, I'm glad I got to see it."

"Please," Lensky said, "tell me you *didn't* hang around within the blast radius just to see what happened. I always thought you were the one member of the Mathematical Mafia who wasn't actively suicidal."

"I'm not," Colton assured him. "Thing is, that was the hell of a long way to jump, and there wasn't anybody waiting for me with a box of doughnuts. I was kind of shaky and after I dropped the bomb, well, I tried to teleport just far enough back to be safe. Misjudged the distance slightly, that's all."

"And then?"

"That's all. I dropped the thing, I skedaddled, it cleared out some buildings Dad had been talking about pulling down."

"All of which would have taken less than ten minutes."

"I was *way* too shaky to teleport back. Or to teleport anywhere, actually. Bud – my brother – came out in the Rover to find out what made the noise, and he had to look at *all* the damage for himself. Finally he gave me a ride back to the house and I talked Janaelle into fixing me something to eat so I could get back here. Didn't want to take the time to wash up and change, I figured y'all would be worried. Kind of a pity I had to dump the bomb right away," he said, "there are plenty of little towns around there that would only be improved by a good bomb. Trouble is, we'd need to get the people out first. Good thing about the old barn site, wasn't nothing but a few tumbleweeds occupying it. Maybe some coyotes. No loss. In fact, saved the farm some money. Not that Bud… oh, well."

*The room he had rented – for cash, under a false name – gave an excellent view of Allandale House. Fortunate that the Center was housed so close to the edge of the campus. Less fortunate, that someone there was cleverer than he'd thought. By ten o'clock he felt sure that the bomb was a failure. He did not make mistakes: the timer had been set to go off at half past nine, the wiring had been perfect – and with a secret fail-safe; anyone who thought he had defused it by clipping the obvious wires would have had a surprise five seconds later. Yet it hadn't exploded early as it would have if some fool tried to defuse it; nor had it exploded at nine-thirty as scheduled. What had they done?*

*He hadn't believed in Shani Chayyaputra's paranormal powers until the grackle spoke to him. Now he had three feathers; one for speech, one for travel, and a new one for a personal shield. And he knew from experience that the first two worked. Very well: logic said that Chayyaputra did indeed have some powers he would have scoffed at two weeks ago. Logic further dictated that someone at the Center also had powers he did not know of. That little bitch who worked with the spook could travel and shield herself. Perhaps they had found the bomb in time; perhaps she or someone else had traveled far away with it, too far for him to enjoy the explosion. That was easier to believe than that he'd erred.*

*At ten o'clock he had seen the world through a red mist of anger at his failure to annihilate the Center with one blow. Later in the day he found, to his surprise, that he was relieved rather than disappointed. He had allowed Chayyaputra to push him into the bombing; that had been the real mistake. Destroying everyone at once, without warning, would not have been a satisfying revenge – especially since they'd never have known what happened to them. Better to stay with his original plan, and take them out one at a time. First some of the bitch's friends; let her know fear. Then the girl; let the spook know despair. And last, the spook.*

*Plastique was all too unwieldy a tool for the beginning of the slow, targeted revenge he intended, though he was thinking of a use for the extra material that might be even more satisfying than killing Chayyaputra. But for the start, he would need something he hadn't brought with him, because it would have been inconvenient to travel with it. A call from a burner phone solved that little difficulty. His preferred tool would be shipped to him overnight, broken down into parts and packed very carefully so that he wouldn't have to sight it in again.*

For the rest of that afternoon – much of it, anyway – Prakash displayed an impressive ability to concentrate. He had evidently decided to apply himself seriously to the Brouwer Fixed-Point Theorem as a key to teleportation. I knew because he kept teleporting into my office, effectively destroying *my* concentration.

"Pick another destination next time," I told him the third time he stepped out of the air in front of my desk.

"It is a limitation," he said, "being able to travel to known places only. Is there not some way to bypass this?"

"There is one thing that has sometimes worked," I said, repressing *but you're too egotistical to be able to use it.* "Sometimes you can teleport to a *person.* But it has to be somebody you know very well and feel very close to. For instance, I once teleported to Lensky without knowing his location. But that was an emergency."

Prakash stared at the window behind me as though memorizing it, turned sideways and vanished.

"*What* did I tell you about picking a different destination?" I snarled five minutes later. This time he'd materialized between my desk chair and the window. Impressive precision, assuming that was what he was aiming for, but why couldn't he pester Ingrid for a change? "Ingrid's office," I said. "Ben's office. Better yet, the supply closet!" Not being quite actively homicidal, I did not recommend that he teleport into Dr. Verrick's office.

"I am not remembering how those places look," he said. "I am remembering your office only, isn't it?"

"Well, go and look at some other place!" I was trying to use TopoCAD to sketch the topological construct Ingrid and Colton had used for their spectacular flying swoops, and since their description hadn't included the parameters this program wanted, I was making a mess of the sketch. Prakash's incursions were not helping.

He actually left me alone for well over an hour after that; long enough for me to admit that it wasn't entirely his fault I couldn't draw the thing, much less visualize it in a way that the stars could power. Colton's adventures had left me disgracefully wobbly. I kept seeing the central room in shambles, with little bits of Lensky and me and everybody else spattered on what remained of the walls.

*Not* the kind of thing I wanted to visualize. I decided to calm myself by some simple imaging: a Möbius strip, a few simple three-manifolds, things like that.

Instead, I found myself listening to Colton, who had been on the phone most of the afternoon. I couldn't make out what he was saying, but he sounded cheerful. So he couldn't have been talking to his family, could he?

Well, yes he could, and now he stepped out of the air in front of my desk. I started a really good snarl before I registered that it was Colton, not Prakash.

"Oh, did I interrupt you?" he said. "Sorry. I just needed to tell someone. Annelise is doing a doughnut run, and Meadow's taken Mr. M. off to the engineering labs to tinker with his latest augmentation."

"A doughnut run this late?" I said, momentarily distracted. It was almost four.

"Prakash," Colton said. "He's worn himself out teleporting around the office. Hasn't he been in here? I've had him twice while I was on the phone, and Ingrid threw a paperweight at him the last time he interrupted her."

"Did she hit him?"

"No," Colton said, "fortunately he teleported out of there just before it landed."

That was Colton being nice again. *I* thought it regrettable that Prakash hadn't paid a price for being such a nuisance.

"He's pretty wiped out now," Colton commented. "Do you think we should give him a set of the stars?"

*No.*

Oh, well. At least he was being a nuisance legitimately, in the pursuit of research and understanding, rather than wasting all our time telling us that we couldn't do what we had done.

"Was that what you came to tell me?"

"Oh, no." Reminded of his news, Colton beamed at me. "I've been talking to Bud. He's decided that whatever I'm doing here is worthwhile after all. I'm not sure," he added, "whether it was me disappearing and then calling Janaelle from here hours before he thought I should have reached Austin, or all the money I saved the farm by demolishing those old buildings. But I... didn't mention to him that the demolition was actually the work of a bomb. If he gives me credit for doing it with topological magic, so much the better. I'm in good with the family again!"

"Mmm. Tell you what, though, if you're taking credit, you'd better get to work on finding a way to do it topologically. He may want you to repeat the trick."

Colton wilted slightly. "I hadn't thought of that. What do you think would work to blow up a building?"

I confessed that nothing occurred to me offhand, and suggested he consult with Ben, who was the most ingenious of us at finding new applications. "And if you think of something, try it *without* stars first," I added. "I don't want to try and explain to the Allandale House trustees how we happened to destroy part of their building."

Colton glanced at his watch. "It's late, anyway. I'll get with him first thing tomorrow, if I don't think of anything tonight. And we'll work outside!"

"Don't concentrate so hard you get frostbitten!"

"In *Austin*?"

A good point. It was cold, and the Weather Underground was predicting snow flurries, but that was unsupported optimism. We hadn't seen snow in Austin since my sophomore year, and it hadn't stuck to the ground then. (The city and university shut down anyway. The roads *might* have been icy.)

I was stacking my notes and reference books, preparing to go home – well, to Lensky's via a stop at Pam's to see Andy – when Prakash stepped out of the air again. His chiseled features were slightly less intimidating with glazed sugar on his lips and a smear of chocolate on one cheek.

# 18. The reflexes of the average topologist

"I take it you've refueled?" I looked at the chocolate smear.

"Nobody was telling me teleporting would do *that*!"

I thought back over the few things he'd allowed me to tell him. He was right. His experiences Thursday night wouldn't have given him any warning; even if I hadn't had the stars, I was strong enough now to zip around campus without fainting. And the one time he'd assisted enough to sense the in-between, I'd done most of the heavy lifting. He got the exhilaration and the heightened libido, but not the exhaustion.

"Fair enough," I allowed. He was leaning against the bookcase, looking tired even after the doughnut fix. "Sorry about that. I don't think any of us were expecting you to do so much this afternoon, though."

His face assumed my least favorite look and the one we'd seen the most of: smug superiority. "This is only what you should be expecting of *cum laude* M.A. from Tata Institute."

He was definitely not getting a set of stars any time soon, not if I had any say in the matter. He was insufferable enough without the power boost they would confer.

And rather than going away, he seemed to have settled in comfortably with one elbow on the bookcase. "Why there is not even one chair for visitors in here?"

"To discourage visitors," I said, hoping he would take the hint.

I should have remembered that Prakash was impervious to hints. In fact, impervious to just about anything short of a cast-iron skillet to the head.

"ISA, Indian Student Association, sponsors *Dil To Pagal Hai* this week."

"Dilto pagalay? What's that?" It sounded like some kind of exotic food, and our trip to the Indian cafe last week had exposed me to quite enough Indian cultural enrichment for now.

"Dil, to, pagal, hai," he said, emphasizing each word. "Meaning 'This Heart is Crazy.' Classic Bollywood film with Shah Rukh Khan. You should see it. Madhuri Dixit plays Pooja and Akshay Kumar plays Ajay."

"Never heard of any of them. Who's…" I tried for the shortest name… "Puja?" *Oops, mistake, you asked a question, he'll never go away.* You see, my reputation for surliness is undeserved; I'm actually way too polite.

"Pooja is name of girl in film," Prakash said. "She makes one big mistake, she accepts Ajay's proposal and introduces him as her betrothed before she realizes that she and Rahul are meant to be together. Rahul is played by Shah Rukh Khan, long time Bollywood heart throb. Some of my friends say I look like Shah Rukh Khan, only taller. And younger, of course. You should see this film, Thalia."

"Um, maybe. I'll tell Lensky about it, maybe he'll want to stay on campus and watch it some time." And maybe pigs would fly and grackles walk. I couldn't see him passing up a rerun of *Burn Notice* for a song-and-dance spectacular. In Hindi. For that matter, I was pretty sure that watching my personal spook yell at the scriptwriters of a spy show was more entertaining than a Bollywood musical. In Hindi.

Prakash went on pointlessly elaborating on the plot of this movie, which sounded significantly more complicated and drawn-out than – oh, than an American soap opera, or even than my last informal report on Center proceedings during fall semester. All he accomplished was to cement my decision not to bother with the film. Well, he also managed to wear out my stock of politeness.

"I'm sure it's a great film," I interrupted him as he expatiated on Pooja's epiphany about Rahul being her true soulmate, "but I want to hitch a ride with Lensky this afternoon, and he doesn't like being kept waiting." Two lies and one half-truth. I thought the film was probably totally sucky, and Lensky has the patience of a spook on surveillance when waiting for me. But I did want him to drive me home, that much was true; after today's excitements, I wanted to revel in the fact that he was whole and uninjured, not spattered over the walls of Allandale House.

"I just wanted to be with you," I said in the car when Lensky questioned my decision. "What's so strange about that? And why are you looking so sour? I should have thought you'd *like* me wanting to hang out." Also, I'd wanted an excuse to brush off Prakash. See, I really am polite and thoughtful.

"For one brief shining moment," Lensky said, "I entertained the hope that the bomb scare had inspired you to be more cautious about teleporting."

"I ride in with you *every day*," I said.

"And teleport back."

"Haven't we been over that? Your condo has to be the safest place in all of Austin. We know neither Balan nor Chayyaputra has been there, so if they want to get in they'll have to use the door like everybody else. The *locked* door."

"All the same."

"Can we stop at the market?"

"What for?"

Being almost blown up had had an effect on my appetite. Also, I thought I should do something to compensate Pam for having stuck her with feeding an adolescent boy. "I'm cooking tonight. For us and Pam and Linda and Andy." Taking a pot of chili over to Pam's house would also give me an excuse to check up on Andy without making it obvious I was checking up on Andy.

"*You* are cooking?"

Look, I might not bestir myself that often, but I actually can do a little more than boil water. I just don't like letting people find out in case they expect me to do it on a regular basis. Look at Mom; she'd cooked herself into a corner by regularly providing Dad with the best Greek food in Austin. Not to mention the best baklava in America.

"My specialty," I told him. "Chili and cornbread. Comfort food, perfect for a cold winter day."

"You call *this* cold?"

Well, yes. The temperature was headed downhill from an afternoon high of 40 degrees. It would probably get down below freezing tonight. If below freezing isn't cold, what is?

"Oh, shut up and go charm the butcher out of three pounds of chili cut beef."

"And that is different from ground beef how?"

"Oh, never mind, you can wait in the car. I won't take long."

I couldn't ask him to get any other ingredients without admitting that my "specialty" relied heavily on cornbread mix, canned beans and tomatos, and a pre-packaged "chili kit" of seasonings with instructions on the back of the package.

The condo was *frigid*; he liked to turn the heat off when we left in the morning. I kept my jacket on until the place was warmed up to a livable temperature. By that time the beef was browned and I could dump everything else in and leave it to simmer.

"You're not planning to make the cornbread now, are you?"

"No, I'll do that half an hour before we eat."

"So why are you preheating the oven now?"

"Because I'm freezing!"

"Oh, come here. I'll warm you up."

Our differing attitudes to cold weather were not solely based on the fact that this was the first winter Lensky had spent in a better place than DC or Jersey. Part of it was simply physiological. When he called me a wimp I pointed out that pound for pound, I had more surface area to expose to the cold than he did. He was stocky, muscular, compact; a body type that had probably evolved over centuries of Polish winters and had only been encouraged by growing up in New Jersey. Also he was considerably larger than I was.

Sharing a bed with Lensky in the winter was kind of like cuddling up to my own personal heater, only more interesting. This evening, for instance, he thought it was funny that I dove under the duvet before even thinking about taking off anything but my shoes. But he also found it entertaining to talk me out of my clothes, one item at a time.

I rather enjoyed that part, too.

What with one thing and another, we didn't get around to calling Pam and offering chili until she had already taken Linda and Andy to Sonic. Oh well, it would be just as good tomorrow, which wasn't forecast to be any warmer. And my brief chat with Andy reassured me; he sounded as happy as could be expected.

Of course, he was skipping school, which didn't make me quite as happy as it did him, but I decided to worry about it another day. Tonight was devoted to celebrating the fact that both Lensky and I were still alive. And he celebrated that fact with impressive enthusiasm.

Over a late meal of chili and cornbread, though, I started thinking about Andy's problems again. There'd been something Colton had said...

"Brad, did Colton Edwards talk to you this afternoon?"

"Only when he was telling all of us about his adventure. Now that young man is a real addition to the Center staff. None of the rest of you thought that fast."

"Well, topologists aren't necessarily the people you want to look at for a fast response. We're more likely to want to sketch some examples and think about the problem at leisure, alone, without anybody bugging us."

"Thank God that Colton doesn't have the reflexes of the average topologist!"

"Agreed. We owe him. That's why I'm so happy things worked out the way they did."

"You need an explanation for being happy that we weren't all blown to bits?"

"Well. Besides that. You know how his father and brother practically declared him an un-person when he decided to work at the Center rather than going home and applying his business degree to the family farm?"

"I heard something, yeah."

I was momentarily distracted by contemplating the difference between men and women. Annelise and I had heard blow-by-blow descriptions, not to mention moaning and mourning, of every contentious interchange Colton had had with his family during last semester. He hadn't even gone home for

Christmas. Lensky and Ben had sailed past all the wrangling without giving it more than passing interest.

"Well, it looks like the bomb has produced a happy ending for Colton. He told me his father and brother were super-impressed by seeing some of what he can actually do since starting at the Center. And he didn't even fly! Just teleporting was enough to change their minds. Well, that and flattening some dilapidated old buildings; he let them think that was applied topology too." I swirled a bit of cornbread in my bowl to soak up the last bit of chili. "It made me wonder... what would happen if I showed *my* father what I've been doing?"

"Apart from rendering yourself liable to major legal penalties?"

"Are you going to try and put Colton away for twenty years?"

Lensky scowled at me. "No, but don't take that as a precedent! Nobody saw him, and anyway he was *saving your life*. You don't have an excuse nearly as good."

"Saving Andy's life?"

"I fail to see how your father's having an improved attitude towards *you* would change Andy's situation."

I had a feeling he was right.

"And Colton incidentally saved the farm a bunch of money while he was saving all of our lives. I guess that might have had something to do with the reconciliation."

"You think?"

I decided to give up thinking. "Do we have any ice cream left?"

"I thought you were freezing!"

I batted my eyelashes at him. "You warmed me up *very* well. Is there any of the cherry chocolate fudge cookie chunk?"

Lensky made some remarks about the propensity of women to mess up perfectly good ice cream with unnecessary additives. I pointed out that I had no problem with his ascetic bowl of plain vanilla as long as I got cherry chocolate fudge cookie chunk when I wanted it.

"Plain vanilla is more adaptable to other uses," he said, and mentioned a use that might indeed be very interesting... come summer. There was no way I was going to let him apply ice cream to any sensitive parts in this weather.

# 19. Vlad the Impaler on voicemail

The next morning was magic.

Weather Underground had redeemed all their previous errors by getting this one right. Overnight we'd had two inches of snow that, amazingly, didn't melt. More snow was falling now. I looked out the windows and dove back under the duvet.

"It's time to get up," Lensky mumbled, throwing an arm over me.

"Why? We're not going anywhere. *Nobody* is going anywhere today."

"Huh?"

"Snow," I said.

In Austin that one word says it all, but I was forgetting that Lensky's idea of winter had been set in New Jersey. Not to mention D. C., Romania, and other exotic locales.

"So?"

"The city will be shut down. University too."

"You're kidding!" He was getting more alert. I didn't *want* to be alert.

"Oh, check the Internet. Austin is *closed*. Nobody can go anywhere." With, okay, the exception of research fellows at the Center for Applied Topology. But Lensky didn't want me teleporting into the office, right? So I had as much excuse as anybody else to sleep in.

My little cave under the duvet started to get colder as soon as Lensky removed his big, warm body. I heard him tapping on keys and muttering to himself. "City offices. Public schools. The university…. What's wrong with you people? Haven't you heard of snowplows?"

I stretched and considered the advantages of getting dressed. I'd have preferred to get warm against Lensky, right here under the covers, but it seemed that wasn't going to be an option.

"Brad, the city doesn't *have* snowplows. What we have is a couple of guys with trucks full of sand. They go around sprinkling it on overpasses and bridges until they run out. And they don't have anywhere near enough to cover even the major roads."

He tapped for a few more minutes, muttering about feckless Southerners, and finally pulled on a pair of pants and padded out to the living room.

I followed him after dressing appropriately for the weather, which involved a lot more clothes than Lensky was wearing. Leggings under my skirt, sweatshirt over the T shirt. And there'd be another layer or two if anybody forced me outside.

The world outside our windows was strangely silent. As I'd tried to explain without actually waking up, nobody in Austin knows how to drive on snow and ice. And we don't need to learn because even an inch of snow on the ground shuts this city down.

Lensky had laid and lit a fire in his hitherto pristine fireplace and was sitting on the carpet, leaning back against the couch, watching the flames. Outside the two tall windows flanking the fireplace, puffy white snowflakes drifted down soundlessly.

He was still shirtless. I'm not very observant or social before the first cup of coffee, but I did notice that and appreciated the viewing pleasure. After getting coffee I came back to the living room and sat on the floor right in front of him, where I could lean back and use that well-muscled chest the way he was using the couch.

He made a superb back rest: firm, warm, and self-adjusting. After I was settled, he put his arms around my midriff and made a couple of friendly noises that weren't quite speech and so didn't require answers. I sipped my coffee and watched the flames while I waited for the caffeine to start my brain working again.

"I wonder what everybody else is doing?" Lensky said after I got my second cup of coffee.

"Everybody else as in our friends and colleagues? Or as in Sandru Balan and the Master of Ravens?"

"Oh, the first. Since everybody else is taking the day off, I'm going to give myself a day off from worrying about the bad guys."

"They're probably sleeping in," I said, "since they didn't have to wake up at the crack of dawn to explain snow days to somebody from the frozen North."

\*\*\*

Annelise and Ben, both familiar with Austin, didn't waste any time or energy checking out the list of closings; they knew what snow on the ground plus more falling out of the sky meant. What interfered with their sleeping in was Mr. M.

"What, he didn't take the snow as a sign that it was time to hibernate?" I asked when I heard this. Ever since October, whenever I asked him to do something he claimed I was ruining his hibernation and demanded coffee.

"I *wish*," Annelise said. "I think he finds us boring. And he claimed the weather was interfering with his streaming music and videos, so he wanted us to do something to entertain him."

I tried to restrain the grin. "What, your usual activities aren't entertaining enough?"

Annelise indicated that, like me, she felt somewhat uncomfortable doing *that* under the observation of a sarcastic, three-thousand-year-old turtle/snake mage.

"And what's worse," she sighed, "he got into the coffee, and you know what he's like *then*."

I did indeed. Hyper was an inadequate description.

They had finally induced him to go back to sleep, but Annelise thought their means *might* have been a mistake.

"We still had some of Dr. Verrick's champagne left from the housewarming party..."

As I remembered, at that party Mr. M. had enjoyed a saucer of champagne without becoming much more difficult than usual. "How much did it take to put him to sleep?"

"More than he could possibly put away," Annelise said. "Considering that he's only a head and a neck and three feet of prosthetic snake body… where *does* he put it all? He killed a bottle all by himself – well, neither of us felt like drinking champagne over breakfast – and it took him a while to go to sleep. First he sang." She shuddered. "Lia, you haven't lived until you've heard him crooning 'Rum and Coca-Cola' in that croaky voice of his. And he knows *all* the words! 'Since the turtle come to Trinidad, He got the girls all goin' mad.'" She imitated his creaky voice.

"I don't think that's *quite* how it goes."

"Yes, well, he doesn't sound much like the Andrews Sisters either."

***

Jimmy and Ingrid were similarly making the best of a snow day. So, eventually, was Colton, but he had to work harder for it. He tramped over to Meadow's place over snow and ice, and his feet skidded out from under him twice before he remembered that he didn't actually have to touch the slippery surface beneath him. For the rest of the way he pioneered extremely low-altitude flight, staying so close to the top layer of snow that anybody who happened to see him wouldn't be quite sure he was flying.

The absence of footprints might have been a giveaway, though.

Once at Meadow's apartment building, he flagrantly violated at least six major clauses and several terrifying fine-print injunctions by flying up to her third-floor window and throwing snowballs at it.

"Come out and play in the snow!" he called when she came to investigate the noises.

"You're insane!"

That was all either of them would say about it, and it seemed to me grossly inadequate to explain how Colton persuaded a girl from the Rio Grande Valley to put on six layers of clothing and join him in making a snowman. I wished they'd taken pictures; bundled in all those sweaters and coats, Meadow must have looked like an opinionated fireplug.

He claimed that he'd even persuaded her to clean up her language by telling her that the way she talked was liable to melt all the snow and then they'd have to go to work.

"That made her laugh," Colton said, "and once you get a girl to laugh, everything else is easier."

I asked if he'd helped her warm up after the snow play, but he refused to comment. Well, he's a gentleman.

*Who would have guessed the whole city, including FedEx delivery, would take the day off just because there were a couple of inches of white fluff on the ground? In Bucharest they'd call this a nice spring day. Americans were soft.*

*Unfortunately, he was dependent on Americans to deliver his scoped rifle.*

*And nobody was even answering the phone at the FedEx office; he'd heard the recorded message three times. The first time, he hadn't believed it. The second time, it was beginning to sink in that the soft Americans really thought two inches of snow an adequate excuse for failing to meet their promise of overnight delivery. The third time, he just waited for the message to come to an end so that he could leave a mention of Vlad the Impaler on their voicemail.*

Despite having forced us to get up, Lensky didn't seem to have much to say. He just held me close and ran his hands over me. Not that I objected. Eventually, though, what I was thinking about came out.

"You've stopped having that dream. Do you think that means it's over?"

"Thalia, I stopped having the dream after you agreed to let me drive you to work instead of teleporting into the office. And nothing will be 'over' until Sandru Balan is behind bars."

I sort of knew that was going to be his attitude, but I sighed anyway. "And you couldn't just count on the FBI to do their job and arrest him?"

He made some comments about the FBI which don't belong in an informal report that anybody might read, and anyway, I'm pretty sure the part about rocks for brains isn't literally true.

"If that bomb had killed you, Thalia, I couldn't…"

"But Colton did get rid of it, and everybody's alive, and I don't want to torture myself thinking of things that didn't actually happen!"

"Don't get mad. I was just thinking…"

"Do you *have* to?" I might have started this conversation, but I wasn't enjoying the way it was going.

"About the future."

Well, wasn't that a conversation stopper!

"I'm just happy I still have one," I said eventually. "Aren't you?"

"I want to have one with *you*."

"Oh, you're stuck with me," I said as lightly as possible, "until you decide you don't want to be." Something that terrified me when I thought about it. Last fall we'd broken up for less than a week and it nearly killed me. How had I allowed this man to mean so much to me, so quickly? And how was I going to survive if he ever realized I wasn't all he imagined me to be, but just an ordinary girl with, ok, some extraordinary abilities? I'd vowed to be careful after that, never to take this – or him - for granted.

"I told you last spring," Lensky said, "that you're *always* going to be my problem. I just – hope that's true."

"What, that I'm always going to be a problem for you? Very flattering!" I twisted around to kiss him… and to get out of a conversation loaded with pitfalls. He wanted to talk in terms of *always* and *the future.* Those words frightened me. If I took him too seriously, I might forget – oh, to be careful. To live in the moment. To be prepared for the inevitable end when he decided he wanted a normal life with a normal person.

Fortunately, he'd recovered sufficiently from last night to be eminently distractible, and I put everything I had into the distraction.

# 20. Praise the Lord and pass the ammunition

On Wednesday the snow was gone and everything seemed to be back to normal. Ben and I finally had a chance to work on the constructs that Colton and Ingrid had developed for flight. We even managed to glide along the hall that connected offices on the private side, a good two feet above the floor, until Dr. Verrick destroyed our concentration by throwing his door open and requesting that we stop giggling and swooping like flying toddlers. I think he enjoyed seeing us crash to the floor. Two feet wasn't enough of a fall to hurt us, but our egos were badly bruised.

With an acid suggestion that we concentrate on how to exit flight mode without crashing, he retreated back behind his closed door to think about whatever he was working on; new ways to torture topology students, probably.

"I'm disappointed in Dr. Verrick," I told Ben, very quietly, while we were sitting on the hall floor examining our bruises. The physical ones, that is: his knee, my elbow and chin.

"Why? He wasn't any grouchier than usual."

"That line about flying toddlers? Lensky used it first, remember? I always thought Dr. Verrick's invective was *original*. Now I learn that he isn't above plagiarizing spooks."

He wasn't above eavesdropping, either.

"Miss Kostis, I suggest you contemplate the possibility that your hi-jinks might inspire the same comparison in two different minds. After which you might spend some time bringing our new intern up to speed, rather than disrupting the office by floating and fluttering to no purpose.

"Mr. Sutherland, I have not yet seen your report on progress in the problem of Riemann surfaces. You *have* progressed beyond using the images for random fire-starting, have you not? No? Then perhaps your creativity would be better applied to that problem."

Having startled us and removed a few strips of skin, he went back to his office and slammed the door again. Ben took himself off to fiddle with Riemann geometry, and I sighed and invited Prakash to practice Camouflage. The good thing was that he picked it up immediately; within half an hour he had mastered the visualization of an open cover on an imaginary surface that allowed him to look like a slightly blurred copy of whatever was directly behind him. The only problem that I could see was that learning our techniques so fast wasn't going to do anything to reduce his overpowering self-satisfaction. Oh well, if he got too bumptious I could always ask Ben to share his work on Riemann surfaces, which, as Doctor Verrick had mentioned, still had an alarming tendency to produce fire rather than the cool light Ben had been aiming for. Either Prakash would have to confess himself stumped too, or he'd figure out how to make light; either result would be fine with me.

I thought out that little plan after sending him out to the break room to recover from the morning's exertions with a quick sugar hit. We were going to have to show him the stars soon. I just hoped we could knock off some of the towering egotism first. We'd learned by experience that careless handling of Mr. M.'s Babylonian stars could get us in all sorts of trouble, from disappearing buildings to involuntary time travel. I didn't think Prakash was ready to be careful enough yet.

I was sure of that when he demonstrated misuse of his two new abilities by sneaking back into my office. I was flipping through some of my notes and thinking about the bomb disposal problem. Specifically, about Colton's promise to get together with Ben and try to find some topological way to accomplish what a pack of C-4 had done to those outbuildings on the farm. They seemed to have forgotten that plan after the snow day. Would it be a good idea to prod Colton on it? Or could that project safely wait until it was warm enough for them to work outside, preferably in a large vacant lot?

I'd just about decided that it could when I noticed that the right side of my bookcase was blurred to the point that I couldn't read the titles of any books. I rubbed my eyes and observed that the whiteboard beside the bookcase was also blurry. Fortunately, there was a textbook that I wasn't all that fond of on my desk. I threw it at the bookcase; the blur disappeared and resolved itself into Prakash, rubbing his arm and complaining that I didn't need to be that aggressive.

"It's not nice to sneak into your colleagues' offices," I said sweetly. "But as long as you're here, would you like to tell me how you achieved a seamless transition from teleportation to camouflage?"

He widened his eyes. "What, doesn't everybody do it that way?"

"What way would that be?"

"Do not be angry, Thalia. I wanted to see you only."

"Don't you have anything else to do?" I felt I'd done quite enough mentoring for one day. He could go and pester somebody else while I got back to work on flying half as well as Colton and Ingrid already could.

"Nothing important," he said, taking his usual pose with one elbow on the bookcase. "Tell me about yourself, Thalia."

"I am impatient to get back to work. That's all you need to know."

He blinked. "Ben told me that asking a girl about herself *always* works."

"Yes, well, it works for him because it's always true. Once he gets interested in a girl, he develops a laser-like focus on her. Did," I corrected. "He's only focusing on Annelise now."

"Sometimes I do not understand you, Thalia."

"Most of the time, it seems. Let me try it in words of one syllable: Go. Away. Get somebody else to mentor you for a while." *And leave me alone to practice flying.*

"Two."

"What?"

"'Away' has two syllables. You really wish me to stay, isn't it?"

"No, Prakash. It isn't."

"Why do women never admit what they are desiring? It is all right, Thalia. No one could object to two colleagues talking in the office. Even the door is open."

"If you'd leave, I could fix that."

"I understand the struggle in your heart. It is just like Ayesha in *Maine Dil Tujko Diya*. She is thinking she must marry Raman, but she is falling in love with Ajay. Raman uses his underworld connections to have Ajay beaten up and nearly killed, but Ajay recovers and marries Ayesha despite all dangers. This man Lensky doubtless is having similar unsavory connections but I am not being swayed by fear."

"You will have something to be afraid of if you keep hitting on me."

"I have told you. I do not fear Lensky or his underworld connections."

"Fine. But you should be afraid of *me*. Has anybody told you yet about the Toad Transformation?"

Prakash blinked but made a quick recovery. "I am thinking there is no such transformation. It would violate the conservation of matter and energy, isn't it?"

"Not if it turns you into a *very large* toad." If he would just go away, maybe I could find some bit of topology that really did turn people into toads. It would be a continuous function...

Prakash made a dismissive gesture. "You would not do that, even if you could."

"What makes you so sure?"

"Girls are squeamish about toads. You do not wish to have a six-foot toad in your office, no? You are just playing a game, trying to be...what is it? Oh, I remember!" He snapped his fingers. "Hard to get, isn't it?"

"Sure," I said between clenched teeth, "and the next move in the game is sending you to a consciousness-raising seminar about sexual harassment."

"Eve-teasing?" Now he looked wounded. "But this is nothing like that. This is true love! I am waiting for you to understand that only, just like Ajay had to wait for Ayesha's love. In time you will see that this Lensky is a mistake. He cannot even understand the work you do!"

That had horrible echoes of the break-up last fall, when I discovered just how vulnerable Lensky was to that line of talk.

"Get out," I said. "You happen to be talking about the man I..." Oh, come on, it shouldn't be that hard to use the word. "The man I... I... *love.*"

"That was hard for you to say, isn't it?"

"That has nothing to do with you!" I left my desk, grabbed his free hand, and teleported us through to the public side of the office. On my way back I visualized the imaginary Möbius strip I was walking as bursting into flames and turning to ash behind me.

Apart from those minor contretemps, Wednesday morning was peaceful enough. We didn't return to high drama mode until lunchtime.

Ingrid and Colton had brought sandwiches, both making fun of the rest of us wimpy Austinites who thought today was cold. Ben, Annelise, Lensky and I were going down to the Burrito Factory, because their pork in green chile seemed like an appropriate response to this clear, cold day. As it happened, we never got there.

Between Allandale House and the Drag, the grackles attacked. Fluttering and lunging, they seemed to be everywhere, with claws and beaks used as weapons. If that doesn't sound like much of a problem, you try fighting off two dozen claws and a dozen beaks while being grackled at. Loudly. I ducked and swatted randomly overhead, as did my companions. I heard Lensky cursing. He seemed to be farther off. When the wings beating around my head temporarily disappeared, I saw that he was no longer next to me. Annelise and Ben were even farther away.

We were being *herded* to separate spots. And if that was what the grackles wanted, we should do exactly the opposite. I raised a shield tight to my body, then slowly expanded it to give me a couple of feet of grackle-free space all around me. Ben could do the same thing if he thought about it; then we'd have to protect Annelise and Lensky, who were both still ducking, cursing, and flailing at the pestiferous birds with both hands.

So was Ben. Deplorable! I wanted to protect Lensky, but I headed for Ben first, to tell him to for pity's sake shield at once!

*The roof gave him an excellent view of the area in front of Allandale House. The first four people to come out for lunch were too close together; holding the feather for speech, he told his grackle companion that he wanted a swarm of grackles to descend on the targets and separate them. It was no part of his plan to fire randomly and take a chance at hitting the wrong person.*

*The clouds of attacking grackles temporarily hid all his targets. Suddenly there was a clear space around one of them. The wrong one for today. All the same, he enjoyed placing the cross-hairs of the scope over her face.*

*"Not yet," he said, "not quite yet, my dear."*

*But having sighted her made him feel quietly confident, as though he had placed his mark on her. He could have killed her; her life was his now, even though she didn't know it yet.*

*She should have at least a day to know fear and loss before he took her out. A week would have been more satisfying, but the risks of being caught would rise to an unacceptable level.*

*To start off the campaign, he chose a different target; he would start with her best friend. Coincidentally, the grackles were backing off this one too, as if they knew he wanted a clear shot. Perhaps they did. He centered the cross-hairs of his scope on the man's forehead and fired.*

"Ben!" I shouted as I plunged through the clouds of grackles. A good thing our shields didn't block sound. "Ben! *Manifold!*" That was the key-word we'd worked with, visualizing the covered manifold and enabling it as soon as we heard the word.

We hadn't rehearsed that for some time, but Ben's reflexes were still excellent. He had his shield up less than a second after hearing the key-word, and as I watched he did as I'd done, extending it outward from his body and forcing the grackles away. Then he turned to Annelise, and I was free to shield Lensky.

It was a good thing we didn't have to talk much, because the cawing and crowing of the grackles drowned out nearly every other sound. Every sound except …the crack of a rifle. Were we all shielded? Yes – but a grackle fell dead from the whirring mass of birds.

That was when Ingrid and Colton decided to take a hand. Not that I could see them; it was what I *heard* that made me look up at the third-floor windows.

Mr. M.'s croak was unmistakable. And it appeared that he could turn up the volume as much as he liked.

There is nothing quite like hearing, "Off we go, into the wild blue yonder," sung by a synthetic turtle-robot, invisibly swooping down on you.

A handful of little stars suddenly appeared, as if someone had thrown them past the invisible boundaries of a camouflage sphere. They struck down grackles and then zoomed away from us again, disappearing where the side of Allandale House looked blurry. Three or four such attacks, and the grackles decided unanimously that they would much rather be perching in the trees.

Mr. M. sang that they were diving down to attack from under and lights flashed among the trees, lighting up branches and birds much as we'd seen the workers for Texas Bird Services doing. The points of light wobbled, spiraled in and out, shook, disappeared and reappeared. Mr. M. segued into "Praise the Lord and Pass the Ammunition." From the sound of it, Ingrid and Colton were flying around the trees.

More lights flashed, this time at the tree nearest us. A clump of grackles departed at high speed and Mr. M. started the second verse.

"All aboard..."

Two more trees lost their burden of grackles.

The rifle cracked again and somebody up in the camouflaged sphere cried out.

Damn! Lensky and I were shielded. Annelise and Ben were shielded. Colton and Ingrid.... Maybe not. Who'd been hurt? I squinted at the blurred bit of sky and thought it might be moving back towards Allandale House.

Mr. M. switched to "Coming Home on A Wing and a Prayer," and the blur headed for an open third-floor window.

The blur disappeared and a moment later somebody slammed the window down, mercifully dampening most of the musical croaking.

Ben and I teleported up to the third floor of Allandale House without discussion and without worrying about witnesses, dragging Lensky and Annelise with us. We found Jimmy standing over Ingrid and pressing a red-stained paper towel to her shoulder. A moment later Colton clumped out of the bathroom with a wild look in his eyes. "Doesn't this place have a first-aid kit?"

"My desk, bottom right-hand drawer," said Annelise.

While Annelise did things with liquids and bandages, Ingrid groused at Colton. "And we *could* have carried on, too." She seemed to have got the last song stuck in her memory. "Ow! That stings!"

"Hold still!"

"But you were too scared of somebody shooting at something he couldn't even see! Ouch! Annelise, you're not scrubbing a floor!"

"Seems like a reasonable thing to be afraid of," Ben said.

"I didn't turn back because I was afraid of getting shot," Colton said. "Not exactly. I was more afraid of what Jimmy would do to me if I didn't bring you back in one piece."

Annelise told Ingrid not to be a baby, and assured the rest of us that the only damage she'd suffered was a long graze on her upper arm. It did not surprise me to learn that Annelise's father had insisted she take a first-aid class as well as learning self-defense from an ex-Mossad agent. Clearly a sensible man, he hadn't counted on the university to teach her anything useful.

The grackle battle had been a joint effort. Colton did Flight, Ingrid did Camouflage and threw stars, and Mr. M., wrapped around Ingrid's waist, deployed his new augmentation to spread shock and awe among the grackles.

They hadn't had anyone to do Shield.

"So what's the new weapon, Mr. M?"

"Narrow beam lasers," Mr. M. said from Annelise's desk after he slithered off Ingrid. "*Quadruple* lasers, on retractable gimbal mounts." He extruded the tiny lasers on their mounts and painted dancing lines of light on the far wall.

Meadow had really outdone herself this time.

"What powers the lasers?" Jimmy asked.

Mr. M. sank limply down onto the desk. "Coffee," he said in a broken whisper, "I need coffee…"

# 21. A surrender with honor

Prakash got to play teacher that afternoon, showing us how he'd combined teleportation and camouflage into a single, fiendishly complex visualization. It wasn't easy to replicate. Every time one of us attempted and failed, I could sense his ego swelling. By the end of the day he was all but unbearable.

By then Ben, Ingrid and I were all able to teleport short distances and arrive inside Camouflage. Colton was still struggling with the visualization, but I suspected he was going to stay until midnight if that's what it took to get it right. Combining these two paranormal effects was going to be *extremely* useful; teleporting within Camouflage removed the risk of being noticed when we stepped out of the air at our destination.

"I told you he could make a valuable contribution to the Center," Dr. Verrick said as he left for the day.

He took the stairs one at a time, cautiously. Any of us could have whisked him down to the first floor. But when Ben first hinted at that option, Dr. Verrick had made caustic comments about Boy Scouts helping little old ladies across the street.

I think we all dreaded the day when he could no longer get up the stairs to the third floor on his own. Would he let us assist him then?

Maybe it would never happen. In theory everybody got older, but in practice Dr. Verrick seemed to have achieved stasis at… seventy? Ninety? A hundred and ten? Today he looked exactly as old, and walked exactly as cautiously, as he had when I was in the first year of Honors Topology.

Oh, well; we'd just have to burn that bridge when we came to it.

I rode home with Lensky, having burnt a *lot* of energy in the Grackle Battle and the subsequent hands-on tutorial. I may have said something to that effect to him; he detoured past Mandola's and loaded up on things like grilled chicken and sliced provolone and fresh-baked ciabatta.

"Do you think that'll keep you alive until dinner?" he asked as I built a sandwich out of these ingredients.

"I thought this *was* dinner," I said, somewhat inelegantly, through a mouthful of sandwich.

"I want something hot," Lensky said. "We'll go out later. Always assuming the *entire city* doesn't shut down on account of nasty-looking dark clouds, or a sprinkle of rain, or whatever."

He was really having a hard time with Austin's attitude towards snow and ice.

"In that case," I said after I'd inhaled most of the sandwich, "maybe I'll just take an hour and drop in on the family."

Lensky's eyes narrowed. "It's Wednesday."

"I am aware of that."

"You never visit your family except for the obligatory Friday night dinner, and not then if you have the shadow of an excuse. And you never go without half an hour of grousing and grumbling first."

"I'm worried about Andy." We'd been keeping in phone contact, and he sounded remarkably contented with his situation. As for Pam, she insisted she was delighted to give house room to this tall, handsome boy. But he couldn't just stay there, conquering the higher levels of his video games and missing school. Could he?

"And you've figured out how to reconcile him with your father?" One blond eyebrow tilted up.

"I haven't thought of any way to use my abilities to improve the profits of a dry cleaning business, if that's what you mean. I may just have to depend on shock and awe. Like Mr. M. with his new lasers."

Lensky studied my face. "It was being shot at, wasn't it?"

"Huh?"

"Ever since lunchtime you've had that weird, jumpy energy going, like somebody who's just been in a firefight."

He might have a point there. Certainly I'd hardly started to refuel when I started feeling an urge to go somewhere and do something. And I'd had an idea about Dad's shouting. Why had I taken what he said at face value? There *were* other interpretations…

"I'll drive you," he said.

"No! I mean – you don't have to; I can teleport easily."

"You mean, you still don't want to introduce me to your family."

"Well, right now," I said cautiously, "that wouldn't be a good idea, would it? Once they know about you, all they'd have to do to locate Pam would be to look up "Lensky" in the phone book. Also, I might have to break a few little rules about non-disclosure, and it's better if you don't actually witness that."

Lensky rubbed the back of his neck. "By 'break a few little rules,' I take it you plan to tear the agreements you signed into little pieces and stomp on them. All right. I'll stay in the car. That way I won't have to know what you're doing. And then we can go on to Asti, if that's okay with you."

The part about him waiting outside wasn't totally satisfactory, but it seemed like the best deal I was going to get. And the prospect of a dark Belgian beer with dinner at Asti sweetened the pot. I grabbed my shoulder bag, dropped in my secret weapon and the document I'd printed out this afternoon, and shrugged on my jacket.

The shortage of street parking places in my parents' neighborhood forced Lensky to wait nearly half a block away. So much the better. I just might be able to pull this off without letting my two worlds meet. I strolled down the sidewalk, swinging my shoulder bag and projecting – I hoped – calm and competence.

Mom was just clearing away dinner when I came in. She fluttered about heating something for me and I persuaded her not to bother without actually saying that I was being taken out to Asti later. Which would have invited questions about who was taking me and why I didn't bring him in to meet them and so on and so on. Sometimes it's a pain and a half keeping my family and friends separated.

Before Mom whisked them away I saw that there were two empty bottles of Lone Star beside Dad. So the one he was working on was likely his third beer. Good, that should mellow him a bit.

"If you're going to talk about that worthless boy," he growled as I sat down opposite him, "don't bother."

Mom blinked back tears and took refuge in the kitchen.

"I wouldn't dream of it," I said airily, leaning back and crossing my legs. "I *quite* understand that you don't care whether he's ruining his life by dropping out of school."

"His choice."

"Or whether he's hanging out with a bad crowd because he's desperate."

"His home is here and he can come back when he's ready to beg my pardon."

"Or whether he has enough to eat…."

Mom surged out of the kitchen like a force of nature. "*Panagia mou!* Yanni, *I* want to know about my little boy!"

"Too bad," I said, though I had to clench my fists under the table to keep acting blasé. "Dad's disowned Andy. Didn't you hear? He doesn't want us to talk about him."

Dad's hands squeezed the beer bottle until I thought it would break. All his knuckles stood out, white against the ropy muscles of his hands.

"I just stopped by to invite Dad to a friendly game of cards." I pulled the deck out of my purse and riffled the edges of the cards with my thumb. "Pilotta?"

Dad's eyes brightened at the sight of the cards. He was *deadly* at Pilotta and preferred the two-handed version so that, as he put it, "I don't have to put up with my stupid partner's mistakes."

"Just to make it interesting," I said, "why don't we play for a little wager?"

His eyes brightened even more. Mom interjected a note of warning. "Yanni, playing cards for money is *gambling*."

"Well, we won't play for money, so that's all right. I was thinking, just a quick game, three rounds; if Dad wins, I'll tell you where Andy is."

"Yanni, do it!"

"And if I win, Dad will promise to let Andy come back without making a scene. And furthermore he'll never verbally abuse him again."

"What does that mean? You college kids with your funny words," Dad grumbled. But his fingers were twitching with desire for the cards.

I looked him straight in the eye. "You know what it means, Dad. It means you stop telling him that he's not manly enough, stop calling him a faggot because he doesn't have a girlfriend yet, stop calling him a wimp because he doesn't want to go out for football and doesn't get in fights, stop telling him the Marines will never look at him. Is that clear enough, or do I need to write out a contract for you to sign?"

"Hah! You don't need to write a contract, little girl, because you're not going to win. Deal!"

I shuffled and gave Dad and myself each six cards, then flipped one face-up on the table.

"Seven of hearts. Do you accept the trump suit?"

"I do."

I dealt each of us three more cards and the game was on in earnest. Mom had, unprompted, sat down with paper and pencil to keep score.

"Sequence," Dad grunted, and showed the seven, eight, and nine of clubs.

"Carre." I had four tens.

He scowled and I glanced over to make sure Mom recorded my points.

At the end of that round he was ever so slightly ahead, because I didn't want to come on too strong and make him suspicious. Yes, of course I was cheating; there's no way I could beat Dad at Pilotta without cheating. The trick was to make him believe the game was on the level. I stretched and yawned. "I've almost forgotten how to play. Getting it back now, though."

"Huh. You never played so good when you were living here," Dad grumbled.

"Well, I *have* been studying mathematics for six years now," I said demurely. "No wonder I'm better at counting cards."

Dad shuffled the deck. "Play! We'll see how much good your college book learning does against a man of experience."

I won the second round by a healthy margin, enough to inspire Dad to pointed remarks about how I might not do so well if I weren't playing with my own deck.

"The cards aren't marked," I said cheerfully, "but by all means bring out your own deck if it makes you feel better." The beauty of cheating by my methods was that it didn't matter what cards we used. Remember, I'd been practicing small object manipulation while Colton and Ingrid went for showy stuff like flying. I could see through the backs of the cards and I could influence which cards were dealt. It wasn't perfect; Dad still scored plenty of points, and of course, I needed to let him do that so he wouldn't be suspicious. But it was good enough to give me the necessary edge.

I totally trounced him in the third round, and it was so much fun it should have been illegal. Wait, maybe it was; I *had* been cheating, after all.

"I don't believe it," Dad fulminated. "I don't *believe* it. You been practicing with your fancy college friends, Thalia?" He hadn't even waited for Mom to add up the tricks; he knew he was beaten.

"I guess mathematics is more useful than you thought," I said. And so it was; without applied topology I wouldn't have been able to cheat nearly so effectively. "Sign here." I pulled out the slightly crumpled document I'd printed that afternoon. It was nothing more than I'd said I wanted at first: just a promise that Dad would stop abusing Andy in any of the named ways.

Dad grabbed the paper and crumpled it in his fist. "I do not need to sign. I am a man, I have honor, I pay my debts. Tell the boy he can come home." His fingers mashed and shredded the paper and he looked almost uncertain. "Will he?"

"I'll tell him what you said." I couldn't really promise more than that; it was totally Andy's decision whether he'd take a chance on Dad honoring his word. I thought he could; once I got over the automatic cowering reflex that Dad's raised voice caused, I'd begun to suspect that he was hurting much more than he admitted over Andy's defection. The card game hadn't really been about bullying him into no more bullying; it had been a way for him to climb down.

With honor.

# 22. Your very, very short future

*On one level, he was enjoying this game of strike and counter-strike. He didn't know all the topologists' abilities, but then, they didn't know all of his. How long could they continue countering his attacks? Not forever. They would have to win every time. He only needed to win once.*

*On another level, he was getting frustrated. He was not in the habit of losing, and on Wednesday he'd lost two battles at once. Someone among the topologists was evidently powerful enough to shield all of them against bullets. And the grackles, although not completely evicted from the trees around Allandale House, had suffered enough to drastically reduce the number of willing spies he could command.*

*It was time, he thought, to end the game. He was not getting paid for this, and there was a potentially lucrative contract awaiting him in Minneapolis if he got there in time.*

*He spent Thursday morning in painstaking preparation for his final stroke, including setting the grackles to tell him the girl's movements each day. He already knew that sometimes she disappeared from the office before the man drove home, and he had deduced that she was teleporting herself to his place. All he needed was one such occasion, and he would be able to take a full and satisfying revenge.*

*The chance came earlier than he'd hoped, almost as soon as his materials were prepared.*

Thursday was a nice quiet day. I buttonholed Ingrid before Prakash got in and asked her to teach him the basics of Flight. That kept him out of my hair all day and gave me a chance to talk over the results of the card game with Andy. I'd anticipated that he would be reluctant to take a chance on Dad keeping his word, but he was easier to persuade than I'd dared hope. He *was* only sixteen; he wanted to go home as much as my parents wanted him there.

Once again, though, he insisted on doing this by himself. "If I hide behind you, Thalia, what do I do when you leave?" He went home Thursday night and I spent the evening biting my nails until I got a text: "All OK here. You coming tomorrow?"

Ah, the Friday night dinner and disparagement gala at our parents' house. I would have preferred to get my teeth cleaned. But I couldn't duck out of the gathering this week; I needed to see how Andy and Dad were interacting and whether things actually were better.

Friday at the Center appeared designed to shake my belief that anything and everything, up to and including surgery without anesthesia, was preferable to the Friday night family dinner. First, the grackles were back. There weren't as many of them as there had been, but they made up for it with increased aggressiveness. On the way into Allandale House I had to duck and pull my jacket over my head to ward off their beaks and claws, and when I reached the third floor the windows were black with cackling grackles.

"Alamo Bird Services claimed they wouldn't return to a spot they'd been chased out of for over a year," I groused. "How come Mr. M.'s laser attack only discouraged them for *one day*?"

"We'll just have to do it again," Ingrid sighed, "with noisemakers as well as lasers."

Mr. M. brightened. "Cannon! I need cannon! And torpedos, and flash-bangs, and Tomahawk missiles!"

Clearly he'd been streaming too many war movies. I left Meadow to talk him down to an augmentation she could actually build, and retreated to my office to devote some serious thought to Prakash's teleport-and-camouflage trick. Was it something we could generalize to other paired visualizations? Teleport-and-shield would be handy. How would I do that?

It was hard to concentrate with grackles tapping at the window and crapping on the balcony. That might have been the problem, or it might have been simply that I was in over my head mathematically. The way Prakash combined teleporting and camouflage depended on a topological construction I hadn't been familiar with. He did know more math than I did, I had to admit that. Given that he was an ABD – All But Dissertation – and I'd stopped with a bachelor's, it would have been surprising if he didn't.

All the same, I was less than thrilled to find him leaning against my open door when I got back from lunch. I told myself not to assume the worst: he might be there to work, not to hash over old Bollywood musicals I'd never seen and didn't want to.

Within five minutes we were off the subject of mathematics and back to musicals. So much for being open-minded: it didn't work.

"You should watch *Dilwale Dulhania Le Jayenge* some time. In English, *The brave heart will win the bride.*"

"None but the brave deserve the fair," I murmured, temporarily distracted.

"Ah, you have seen it!"

"Nope. I was quoting an English poet." Pope? Dryden? Some dead white guy.

"It is very sweet film. You will like it, Thalia. Simran's father planned when she was born for her to marry the son of his friend whom she has never met. She is good girl, so she agrees to the engagement. But she is also sad that her future is belonging to this stranger, so she begs her father for a month of freedom only, before the wedding. In that month she travels and meets Raj and they fall in love."

So far it sounded exactly like every other Bollywood flick he'd bored me with.

"There is a very moving scene at the end of their journey. He asks if she'd still marry her betrothed if she fell in love with someone else. She does not answer, then the train horn sounds and she turns to go."

"Is that the end?" I hoped.

"No, of course not. Story cannot end until she is with Raj. True love must always triumph. Just like in real life."

If he believed that was true of real life, he was even more inexperienced than I'd suspected.

"Thalia, you are very loyal person. I am thinking that maybe you would feel it your duty to stay with Lensky even after you fell in love with someone else. Just like Simran felt her duty to honor the engagement to her father's friend. But she came to realize in the end that this was wrong."

"Yes, well, here we have one of those inconvenient disconnects between reality and fiction, Prakash. I am *not* in love with someone else."

"When you will be admitting the truth that you are already knowing in your heart?"

One of the truths I had discovered – not, I think, the one he had in mind -was that Prakash's syntax deteriorated when his emotions took over. *My* emotions were about to take over too, and they weren't nice; I was sick and tired of hearing this egotistical oaf pretend he had some special insight into my feelings. I didn't really want to go off on him, though, so I looked for some way to de-escalate.

"Prakash. Please stop thinking in terms of romantic clichés. I am not in love with you. You are not in love with me. Until you went crazy last week you didn't even like me! We are *colleagues*, not a *couple*."

"The heart is crazy, it's true."

Sounded like the title of a Bollywood musical.

"But love will not be denied! Give me one chance only, Thalia. When you know my love, you will realize that you are too good for that fellow Lensky. You should be with one of your own kind."

*Dammit, enough is enough!* He reached for me as my temper took over in a white sheet of flame. I brought the edge of my hand down on his wrist, *hard.* "Not. In. A. Million. Years! Get that through your swollen head, you egomaniac. And never touch me again if you want to keep those fingers!" I was too furious to stay there in my office, between Prakash and the damned grackles. "Ingrid," I shouted through the partition, "tell Lensky I went home early, okay?"

I turned sideways and vanished.

Lensky's condo was so close that teleporting there felt instantaneous. There was no sense of traveling the in-between to improve my mood, so I was still furious when I stepped onto the living room carpet. I clenched my fists and said several Greek words that Dad thinks I don't know. Then I switched back to English to fulminate at greater length. "Idiot! Sex maniac! Presumptous prick!"

"I do hope those words aren't addressed to me," said a cool voice behind me.

I half-turned and caught just a glimpse of a blond head and some black feathers. Then Sandru Balan grabbed me and pressed a smelly rag over my nose and mouth. I started to stamp on his toes and... fell into the darkness.

I felt as if I were swimming upwards through unnaturally heavy, viscous, black water. Except I couldn't exactly swim, because something was constraining my arms and legs. Cords, cutting into me. Who had tied me up and dumped me into the water?

Then I blinked in the light and registered that I was still in Lensky's condo. I felt a momentary relief; then I saw Sandru Balan, kneeling over me with a terrifying smile on his face. I filled my lungs and started to shout for help, but his hand went over my mouth.

"You really do not want to do that," he said.

I twisted my head back and forth, trying to free my mouth, but his hand moved with me.

"Now stop fighting me and let me explain why calling for help is a really, really bad idea. You see, you are wearing a suicide vest. Yes. It is packed with plastique – my contacts in the demolition business have been *most* helpful – and this wire here is connected to the detonator. If anyone comes through that door, thus reducing the tension on the wire, there will be a fatal explosion – well, perhaps not fatal for him, but certainly for you.

"And I am afraid that I cannot allow you to move. The cords binding your arms also tie you to Monsieur Lensky's very sturdy bed. You can feel a bedpost behind you. If you attempt to teleport yourself to some other location, I suspect the bed will be too heavy for you to move. In fact, I am quite certain of it; I tested a similar arrangement personally.

"You may be wondering how I knew that you had arrived here well ahead of your CIA boyfriend. The grackles around Allandale House are not merely a nuisance; I ordered them to keep watch on you and to notify me the first time you came here before he could. It was a stroke of luck that you left so early; now you will have several hours to contemplate your very, very short future. Or – not. You see your cell phone?"

He held it up in front of me.

"This also can send the signal to detonate your so charming vest, the next time someone calls you. Sadly, you do not have much of a social life, so it is unlikely that it will spare you the hours of waiting. Unless…"

He tried to look as if he had just thought of something, but I suspected the entire speech had been prepared ahead of time, including whatever sadistic twist he was about to reveal.

Not that it mattered.

"I do believe that when I summon the grackles to take me away, I shall have them begin by transporting me to the third floor of Allandale House. I shall encourage your boyfriend to telephone you. If I succeed, the wait for your inevitable death will be shortened. But I shall have the delicious pleasure of informing him that he has killed you. Yes. Definitely worth it, don't you think?"

He stood, pulled a grackle feather from his pocket and stroked it. Seconds later, he was at the center of a whirling cloud of grackles; and then they all disappeared, leaving me with a bad taste in my mouth and no idea how to free myself.

I tried anyway.

"*Brouwer*," I croaked, and the image I used for teleporting formed in my mind. But nothing moved; the in-between did not welcome me. The bed weighed me down fatally.

Even if I had been able to teleport, I would still have been wrapped in explosives and at the mercy of a call to my cell phone. I thought over my other paranormal abilities. Flying failed, just like teleporting. I formed a shield repeatedly…*outside* the deadly layers wrapped around me. All my efforts to form a shield between me and the explosives failed.

Camouflage? I couldn't see any way that could possibly be useful.

Telekinesis? I tried, but without being able to touch my stars I couldn't move anything as heavy as my cell phone.

Think, think, *think*! But don't think about your cell phone ringing.

Fire. A last resort, but I was desperate. I pictured the Riemann surface that Ben and I had studied so intently, trying to make it generate light instead of fire, and coupled it with an image of the bedpost behind me.

I thought I could sense flames starting there. A moment later I was sure of it; they were scorching my hands and wrists. Never mind. With my hands free I would be able to grab the cell phone and maybe destroy it somehow, and then I could very carefully get out of this vest, and then I'd figure out how to deal with the door detonator.

My wrists felt as if they were on fire now, and the backs of my hands weren't much better.

# 23. You have just killed her yourself

Since Thalia was no longer there to hear him out, Prakash retreated to his temporary office to fume in privacy. How *dare* she presume to say that he didn't love her? The only possible explanation was that she did not understand love as he knew it (mostly from movies, but so what?). True love was a fire that consumed you from inside. It was the knowledge that you would be forever incomplete without your soul mate. It was a force that transcended all conventional boundaries.

If she thought she loved that spook, it was only because she had not yet known the fire of love. He could understand the man's attraction for her; this Center was a ramshackle affair that might collapse at any minute. It was only natural that a girl with no family to take care of her (she'd never mentioned any family) should be swept off her feet by an older man (certainly over thirty) with a steady, well-paid job.

He could even forgive her. She was simply too inexperienced to recognize the difference between true love and her gratitude for the security Lensky could offer. It was just like Simran's engagement to Kulheet in *Dilwale Dulhania Le Jayenge*, or Ayesha and Raman in *Maine Dil Tujhko Diya*, or Pooja and Ajay in *Dil To Pagal Hai*, or… literature and film were full of stories about mismatched couples, girls who recognized their hearts and their true loves and thought it was too late. (Although nice Indian girls didn't carry their errors to the point of actually sleeping with the wrong man.) But in the end, love always triumphed, and it would for him too. Film had also taught him that the true hero had to be patient, and he might be required to help the girl to recognize her love for him.

Also, having given her virginity to Lensky (surely there had been no other men), she probably thought that she could not love another. Indeed, many men of his acquaintance would reject a sullied dove, a broken flower. But knowing the promiscuity of American girls and her likely inadequate instruction, he could (with a mighty effort) rise above that.

Probably.

All he really needed to do was to take her in his arms and awaken her. He had been too restrained; she might even think him *weak* for all the times he'd meekly accepted her brushing him off.

But how could he do that when she wasn't even here?

He seethed for several minutes before he remembered something she herself had told him. There was a way to teleport without knowing the place you wanted to go. "Sometimes you can teleport to a *person*. But it has to be somebody you know very well and feel very close to."

For him, that would be Thalia! And when he appeared beside her, she would have to acknowledge the strength and purity of his love.

He was alone in his office; nobody noticed when he vanished.

Everybody else was transfixed by the drama in the outer office.

Even though all the windows were closed against the cold, Sandru Balan had appeared in a cloud of grackles that disappeared as he materialized.

"Do you know where your girlfriend is right now?" Balan asked Lensky, self-satisfaction oozing from every pore.

"I *wish* I'd brought Mr. M. today," Annelise mourned.

"Does it matter? I know where *you* are right now."

Balan laughed. "Kill me, and you will never see her again." Actually, the spook would never see her again in any case; if Lensky didn't take this bait, he'd still destroy her when he opened his own front door. But how much more delicious it would be to enjoy his despair and remorse right now!

Two of the other men in the room moved toward him, one moving his lips.

"Stand down, Ben, Colton," Lensky said without looking. "You son of a bitch," he addressed Balan, *"Where is Thalia? What have you done?"*

"Nothing irrevocable... yet. Let us play a little game called 'Find the girl.' If you can call her cell phone, find out where I have put her, and get there before me, she may live. Of course you cannot do that, because I can call upon my servants to transport me there instantaneously, but it might be amusing to see you try."

The spook fished a cell phone out of his pocket and hit one button. Oh, better and better! He had her on speed dial. Of course!

Balan laughed loudly and long.

"You will get no answer – ever," he taunted Lensky. "Do you know why?"

"You've destroyed her phone."

"Oh, no. Far better than that! A call to her phone set off the detonator. I could have set it off at any time, but it was much more satisfying to let you do it. When you go home tonight, you will find the wreckage of your apartment decorated with the bloody shreds of your beloved. You have just killed her, spook. Blown her into tiny pieces. Can you live with that knowledge?"

The man Lensky drew his weapon.

"Oh, don't kill yourself just yet. You've barely had time for me to savor your despair." He laughed again.

*"Stand down!"* the spook said again, swinging his weapon to force the others in the room to stay where they were. He brought it back and trained it on Balan. Oh, this was an exquisite pleasure! He hadn't yet realized that a gun was no threat to a shielded man.

"First," Lensky said in a remarkably steady voice, "I'll kill *you*." The crack of the Glock was deafening inside the room; Balan felt no need to move, but the man he'd attempted to shoot the other day cried out and clutched his arm. Well enough! He didn't care how many people were injured by ricocheting bullets before this Lensky gave up and shot himself.

"Ben?" The spook half-turned.

"Ricochet," the wounded man said. "You can't shoot him, Lensky, he's shielded." He shook off a pretty girl who had run to him. "In a *minute*, Annelise. If his shield is like ours," he told the spook, "it will stop anything that moves as fast as a bullet. Too bad bullets don't *move slow*."

"Indeed." Lensky began walking towards Balan.

"Idiot," Balan mocked him. "Do you think if you're closer the bullet won't move as fast? Guns don't work that way, my friend. You'd do better to turn it on yourself." Although he'd prefer to prolong the man's agony.

He anticipated that when he reached the boundary of the shield the spook would bounce off it, just like his bullet. Instead he continued moving slowly towards Balan.

Suddenly Balan realized three things. His shield was not, after all, totally impenetrable.

The words *move slow* had been instructions to Lensky.

And he didn't – quite – have time to reach into his pocket for the feather that would call the grackles to transport him out of reach.

Lensky did not doubt for a minute that Balan was telling the truth about the trap he'd laid. *This*, and none of the previous episodes, must be what his dream had warned him of. They'd been fools to assume that the magic of the grackles worked just like the topologists' teleportation. That since neither Balan nor Chayyaputra had been inside the condo, it was safe from them. Thalia had teleported herself there, where Balan must have trapped her. By his own careless action she had been killed, destroyed, *shredded*. And the dream had been true: she'd teleported, and he would never see her again.

Loss and grief all but paralyzed him. Balan was right; he had better turn his weapon upon himself. But there was one thing he would do first.

*Thalia, my love.*

*Never again.*

He shut those thoughts away, behind a partition. He dared not think now. There would be time to grieve after he had done this one last thing; and time to end his grieving with a bullet, too.

For a man reputed to be so intelligent, Balan did not appear to realize the danger that approached him until it was almost too late. Lensky was already pushing through the shield. Balan grabbed his wrist and tried to force the gun down. "If you – fire that," he said jerkily, "the bullet will ricochet inside this shield until it lands in one of us, and it's as likely to be you as me. If you want to kill me, you'll have to do it with your bare hands."

"Delighted," Lensky said, and threw himself on the man who had killed his love. He was hampered briefly by holding the gun, but then Balan struck it out of his grasp and it fell to the floor without, God be thanked, discharging. And Balan had made a serious mistake, devoting both his hands to the problem of the gun. Lensky got his hands around the bastard's neck and squeezed. Balan kicked, arched, twisted, struck again at the wrist he'd hit before and escaped his grip. In the next few minutes Balan demonstrated that he was strong, flexible, and a remarkably dirty street fighter. But Lensky outweighed him, and he had learned his own fighting skills on the streets of Trenton. After inflicting more damage – though not nearly enough, not yet - he got Balan to the floor and choked him again.

"Don't kill him!" someone in the room shouted.

Why not?

"*Lensky!* Please, please don't kill him!"

Oh, well. He could wait a few minutes. Lensky squeezed tighter until Balan went limp. He ground his thumb into a nerve pressure point to make sure the man wasn't faking, and then tied him up with his own belt.

During the struggle three long, iridescent black feathers had fallen out of the man's pocket. Lensky picked them up. He didn't know anything about magic, but one of his grandmother's tales floated through his mind. A magic token… Balan wasn't the Master of Ravens. Shani Chayyaputra was. And Balan carried grackle feathers…

Balan twitched and opened his eyes. They were fixed on the three feathers in Lensky's hand. He doubled himself up and lunged clumsily at them.

"I wonder," Lensky said, "what happens if these burn up? Do you burn with them? Ben," he called without looking behind him. "can you set these on fire?"

There was a pause of several seconds during which Lensky had to keep dodging Balan's attempts to reach the hand holding the feathers; then the tips burst into flame and Sandru Balan screamed. Lensky kept his hand clenched around the quills until the feathery part was quite burnt up. He didn't care about getting scorched. To his disappointment, Balan stopped screaming when the fire went out. Worse yet, he appeared to be unsinged.

"I'd have burned them one at a time," Lensky said softly, "if I'd known how it would hurt you."

Balan's shield was gone now. He knew because half a dozen people threw themselves on him and pulled him away from Sandru Balan. "You mustn't kill him now," Ben panted.

"It would be murder," Ingrid said.

"And even Annelise might not be able to explain it away," said Jimmy.

What did it matter?

# 24. I am IIT-trained expert in destruction of small devices

A slit appeared in the air before me, widened until he could step through it, then healed itself.

"Prakash! What are you – oh, never mind. Help me!" My hands were free, but I hadn't managed to burn through all the cords holding me to the bedpost. The cell phone lay on the carpet, just out of reach.

"Thalia! Your *hands*!" He knelt beside me.

"Later! The cell phone – the phone – "

"You want it?"

"If anybody calls my number," I said, "the bomb will go off."

"Ah!" Prakash was on his feet again. "I am IIT-trained expert in destruction of small devices." He brought one of his gleaming black shoes down on the phone with so much force that fragments of the case spattered all over the carpet. "And just to be sure…"

He picked up the mangled phone and disappeared for a moment. "I was putting it in water," he said on his return. "Allow me to assure you that water is inevitably fatal to these devices. It is common hazing of new students to put their phones in the toilet."

"Where did you put mine?"

Prakash's eyebrows rose. "Why, in the toilet, of course. After all, I know by a previous theorem that this will work. Now to free you…"

"Wait!" I said as he dropped to one knee and opened his pocketknife. "The wire." I touched it with one finger. "If it goes slack, that will set off the bomb. I daren't move."

"Hmm." Prakash considered the problem. "The wire is not actually attached to you," he said eventually. "It is attached to the... thing that is wrapped around you."

"The bomb, you mean?"

"Yes. But do not fear, Thalia. I shall extricate you without allowing tension on the wire to drop."

He closed his hand around the wire, two feet from my body, twisted slightly and severed it while using his hold to maintain tension. Then he wrapped the cut end of wire back around his hand. "Now," he said, "we are removing the bomb from your person, isn't it? Slowly-slowly, yes, and I keep the wire tight all the time."

He cut the remaining cords, awkwardly, one-handed. I saw blood drip from the hand that was holding the wire. "You're hurt?"

"This wire is very fine. It is not important. Stand now, carefully..."

With agonizing slowness I wriggled free of the pocketed vest Balan had strapped around me, always careful to maintain the tension on that damned wire. Prakash moved his hand to mimic my movements, and took hold of the entire vest as soon as possible.

When I was out of the thing, he suggested that I trap it under the bedpost. That, I was able to do. And then I found some of the longer bits of cord, tied one to the other bedpost, passed it through the loop Prakash had made in the wire and pulled it taut so that Prakash could finally relax his hold on it.

We were both sweating freely when the process was completed, and I couldn't wait to get away. Prakash's improvised system could fail, or there could be yet another detonating device that Sandru Balan hadn't mentioned.

"We need to get back to the office and warn everybody." But my head was swimming. Being drugged, tied up, and left waiting for imminent death will do that to a girl. Having to generate fire via Riemann surfaces, without the aid of my stars, had also contributed to wiping me out. I didn't think I could visualize as much as a Möbius strip right then.

I slid my fingertips into my right-hand pocket, very gingerly so as not to aggravate the burns – which were now hurting like hell – and drew out a sprinkling of stars clinging to my fingers. I held my hand out to Prakash, who was staring at the tiny blue-white lights sparkling on my fingers.

"Take them," I said impatiently. My hands and wrists were *really* hurting now, and the longer we stayed anywhere near the bomb the more twitchy I got. "You are going to have to do the heavy lifting. I'm not sure I can teleport right now. The stars will add power." When he opened his palm, I tapped my fingers against it and the little twinkling lights formed a miniature glowing cloud in his hand. He looked surprised; I hadn't mentioned how the lights *felt*. (Like a series of very small, friendly shocks, is the best way I can describe it.)

Lensky's bedroom blinked out and we were stumbling at the top of the stairs to the third floor of Allendale House. A slightly rough landing, but give Prakash props for being able to do it at all. The only problem was that I was not quite as steady on my feet as I should have been, and I went down, hard, on one knee.

It looked as if the rest of the Center had been having an interesting time too. Everybody was out in the central room, and most of them seemed to be hanging on to Lensky. When he turned his head to look at us, his face was like nothing I'd ever seen before: dead white. A mask of grief.

"*Thalia?*"

He whispered my name as if he thought he was seeing a ghost.

I scrambled to my feet and registered that beyond Lensky, there was a man lying on the floor. Tall, blond…. Was it Balan?

Lensky shook off the people hanging onto his arms as though they were no more than some dried leaves on his jacket. With three steps he reached me and swept me into his arms, and – I was *not* going to do a girly thing like crying on him. I did some furious blinking and swallowed, hard, before I raised my face to his.

There were tears in *his* eyes.

"I thought you were dead," he whispered. "I thought I'd killed you. Balan came here and goaded me into calling you, and then he said that my call had been the signal for the detonator."

Which, I supposed, accounted for the fact that Sandru Balan was gagged and tied up on the floor, sporting a number of impressive scrapes and bruises. Lensky had collected some marks himself, though I couldn't figure out exactly how he'd scorched his left hand.

"What do we do if he calls the grackles for help?"

Lensky's smile was wolfish. "I think he can't do that any more. I burned the feathers – his tokens from the Master of Ravens." Oh. That explained it.

Prakash cleared his throat. "Thalia has been badly burned," he informed Lensky.

"What? *Where?*" Lensky started running his hands over me.

"Just this, and it's not that bad." I showed him my wrists and the backs of my hands. They were covered with raised, puffy blisters and under that there were streaks of red. "It's, um, not as bad as it looks." I needed to remind myself of that, because they were throbbing and hurting rather viciously by now.

"Balan did that?"

"No!" I said quickly before he could move towards the captive. "No, he just tied me up. I did this to myself. Burning the cords until I could get my hands free."

Ben grinned. "Riemann?"

"Riemann," I confirmed. "At last we're getting some practical use out of your discovery."

Annelise swooped down on us with the first-aid kit she kept in her desk and started working on all three of us. Prakash and Lensky didn't need much beyond antiseptic gel and bandages, but she frowned over my hands. They were looking kind of gross by now. "I think... this is beyond my first aid skills. You really need to see a doctor, Lia."

"In a few minutes. Look, can you just cover the blisters up for now, so they don't get infected? I *have* to know what's been going on here."

They filled me in on everything that had happened since Sandru Balan's appearance. Lensky kept trying to apologize for letting Balan trick him into making that phone call.

"Yes, he told me he was going to do that," I said. "We got lucky with the timing. You must have called right after Prakash destroyed my cell phone. Oh, by the way, be *very* careful going into the condo. The bomb's still there." I described the setup in as much detail as I could. Lensky pulled out his phone and went off into a corner to call somebody.

"It's arranged," he announced on his return.

"Who'd you call?"

"My FBI contact. She'll get the city to arrange a bomb disposal squad and then she'll come here to collect Balan."

"She?" I echoed.

"What's the FBI got to do with it?" asked Jimmy.

"She's a very competent woman… for a Fibbie. And the FBI comes into it because as I've explained before, my agency does *not* have authority to make domestic arrests." The last few words came out through clenched teeth; Lensky hated having to turn his work – or in this case, his captive – over to another agency.

Ben let out his breath. "Good thing Thalia showed up before you killed Balan, then."

Lensky looked wistful, as if mourning lost opportunities. "I'm really not through with the bastard. I don't suppose you would consider untying him and letting me spend some quality time alone with him before the FBI gets here?"

"*No*," said a number of people at once.

"Not unless I get to play too," said Prakash.

Lensky looked at him. "Bhatia. I owe you. But Balan is *mine*."

This conversation wasn't going anywhere good. I sat down at Annelise's desk, rather more abruptly than I'd intended. "Does anybody have an aspirin?" The waves of pain were making me want to throw up, and I really didn't want to interrupt the argument in such an embarrassing way.

# 25. All your nights and all your days

Against my complaints that it was too dangerous to remove two of our working topologists while Balan was still there, Lensky had Ingrid whisk me off to the nearest emergency room before the FBI even showed up. "Face it, Lia," Ben said, "you're not up to doing much right now. If Ingrid can give up seeing the rest of the grand finale to escort you, *you* can damn well accept it graciously."

True.

But I still considered it grossly unfair that I was going to be deprived of the last act, although I had to admit it was worse for Ingrid, having to miss everything just to babysit me. I explained to Lensky that this was totally unnecessary and he reminded me that the Master of Ravens was still free and that I was currently unable to do any applied topology whatsoever.

"I'll recover in a few minutes."

"No, you won't," Lensky said.

"What do *you* know about it?"

"That 'aspirin' I gave you? Tylenol 3."

It took me longer than it should have to work it out. "That's got *codeine* in it."

"And given your reactions to any kind of opiates or sedatives," Lensky said, "you won't be able to apply any topology at all for the next few hours. So let Ingrid take care of you."

"Traitor." I considered screaming at him for drugging me, but it didn't seem worth the trouble; there was a nice fluffy cloud rising around me and although my hands were still throbbing, that seemed to be happening in a universe far, far away.

Ingrid made everybody there swear on *Foundations of Point Set Theory* that they'd tell us everything when we got back. "Preferably with videos," she said, "you all have cell phones, so use them!"

After all that, Annelise told us when we got back, there wasn't actually that much drama. Kate Highman, the FBI agent in charge, showed up with two very large gentlemen who hauled Balan to his feet and walked him out of the office. Lensky went with them.

Everyone relaxed once Sandru Balan was in custody and out of our offices. Chairs were dragged out of personal offices, soft drinks were brought from the vending machine downstairs, and they draped themselves over the chairs in varying stages of collapse.

"Prakash, of course, did not slump," Annelise allowed. "I'm not sure his spine allows that configuration. Also, he felt cheated; indignation probably kept him from collapsing like the rest of us."

"Cheated?"

"It seems that in all the best Bollywood flicks," Annelise said, struggling to keep a straight face, "the girl realizes that the handsome hero who rescues her is really her true love."

"He's delusional!"

"It's all right. Ben explained to him that Lensky's *owned* you since the day he walked into the Center and you're so crazy about him that you don't even see anybody else."

"That's a gross exaggeration." I'm not that easy! It had been a whole week before I fell for Lensky.

Before I admitted it, anyway.

"Then Dr. Verrick came stumping up the stairs and demanding to know why the entire staff of the Center were lounging around like odalisques."

I was momentarily distracted. "Like *what*?"

"I think it means like, a harem girl or something."

"Prakash must have *loved* that."

"You forget. He was the only one not lounging. Anyway, we tried to explain to Dr. Verrick." Annelise shuddered. "I understand now why all you topologists are terrified of the man. It was like when Lensky gets furious at you guys for going off and getting in trouble, only worse. *Much* worse."

"Yeah. Dr. Verrick's critiques could strip paint." They rarely did any structural damage, though.

"Believe me, you and Ingrid are lucky you missed that. He wound up by telling Ben and Prakash to give formal presentations on the applications of topology they used."

"Just as long as the words 'true love' don't enter into Prakash's presentation."

Annelise shook her head. "He's too professional for that. I think you're safe. But, Lia..."

"Yes?"

"He *did* teleport himself to you without knowing your physical location. That... doesn't happen very often."

Ben to Annelise. Me to Lensky. Yes, there was a pattern. You could only teleport to someone you knew and loved.

I guessed Prakash wasn't totally delusional. Not about his feelings, anyway. Only about his having a snowball's chance in hell of detaching me from Lensky.

"He'll get over it."

"I hope so." Annelise didn't seem so sure.


I didn't make it to family dinner that night. The bandages were too conspicuous. I was too tired. And Lensky wouldn't let me out of his sight. But I did talk to Andros on Saturday morning, and he seemed fairly okay with the home situation. That would have to be good enough until my hands healed.

Lensky had to go to D.C. at once, that same Saturday, for some reason connected with winding up this case; either to testify, or to fill in details for his superiors, or to coordinate with the FBI. Because he doesn't talk about Agency business any more than he can help, I wasn't clear on the details. And

I didn't really care, so long as Sandru Balan wound up being put away for a long, long time.

I did mind the agency's keeping Lensky in D.C. indefinitely, though. Quite apart from the regular nightmares about Balan killing both of us, until he came back I would have to actually live in the apartment I nominally shared with Ingrid. That was a sop to his anxiety; after the Tylenol 3 wore off and I got something to eat, I was once again a fully functional applied topologist. But he'd made me promise to stay with Ingrid until he got back. We still didn't know what had happened with the Master of Ravens; all we knew for sure was that Shani Chayyaputra had checked out of the Driskill.

And for my part, I wasn't too eager to try sleeping in the condo again. Lensky's bedroom had become the setting for my nightmares. I didn't know what we were going to do about that. So Ingrid and I rubbed along together much as we used to do pre-Lensky, which is to say, not very well. And he called every day, sounding more and more tired and worn down. I had some ideas on what to do about *that*, but they'd have to wait until he was back in Austin.

Almost three weeks after leaving, he called to announce that he was done in D.C. He didn't sound his usual bouncy and exuberant self, though; clearly he was still tired. He sounded – almost tentative. It wasn't one of his normal modes.

"I'm coming back tonight. Could you..."

"Pick you up at the airport?"

"No, I still don't know exactly when I'm arriving. All the flights that get in at a reasonable hour are full. I'm trying to get on standby, but if that doesn't work... Well. Anyway. I'll probably be *late*. And I was wondering if you'd... um... stay at the condo tonight. I'd just like to know you'll be there whenever I do get in."

"Of course I will," I said before I could chicken out.

When I stepped out of the air into Lensky's living room, the first thing I noticed was that the place smelled slightly of paint. I walked into the bedroom and saw why.

The room had been completely redecorated. It had been a dimly lit cave; now,

173

with the ugly yellowing plastic blinds replaced by a gauze drape, and the overhead light fixture with white wall sconces, it felt light and airy. Instead of Landlady Beige, the walls were now a cool, light green. The new carpet was a darker green. The chest of drawers had been replaced by built-in white shelving along one wall. And the old but sturdy bed was gone, replaced by a simple low bed in a frame with no posts, no headboard, nothing that anybody could be tied to.

I wanted to cry. He'd done all this at long distance, just for me. It must have been hell arranging everything; no wonder he'd sounded tired! In fact, possibly I did cry just a little bit. There were no witnesses, and I'll deny it if anybody ever asks.

Then I washed my face and put the dark teal sheets on the bed. (I'd upgraded his laundry closet some months earlier; the man hadn't known sheets came in any color but white.)

I'd expected to stay awake until he was home, but it had been a long day. I started sinking around eleven and gave up completely at one. I'd brought over a new, very fancy nightgown but discarded that idea too; we were both going to be way too tired to deal with the complex arrangement of straps and laces, and a girl could strangle herself trying to casually whip off that little number. In the end I just crawled between the sheets in my black lace bikini panties and one of his old T-shirts, the kind that's soft and mellow from many washings and always has a faint scent of the owner. Comfort sleepwear.

And I actually slept, which I hadn't quite expected to do. I dreamed that he'd already come home and wrapped himself around me, and that dream changed slowly into the real thing, a warm body at my back and hands sliding under the shirt.

"Can I turn the light on?" he murmured.

"Mm-hmm." He liked to look at me on those dark, dark sheets - and I liked the way he looked at me. When he sat up to switch on the lamp I pulled off the T-shirt and dropped it on the floor.

He looked me over with an appreciative glint in his eye. He was smiling. Grinning, almost. "The black lace panties are icing on the cake. They make you look totally wanton... and delicious." He ran one hand over me from shoulder to pantyline, appreciative.

I was still slightly groggy. "You – how did you *do* all this?" I waved my hand around the room.

"Melted the credit card," he said. "It's amazing what people will do if you pay them enough."

"You – you didn't have to."

"Right. I suppose the scientific approach would have been to bring you over here and calibrate exactly how miserable it made you to be in this room. *Then* hire the decorators. Anyway, I had to do something; some careless girl had scorched a big spot in the carpet." He wrapped his arms around me. "I wanted you here. And I wanted to make it as painless for you as I possibly could."

I was having to blink fast. He thought I was worth this kind of trouble and expense? "It's too much," I said, and my voice, dammit, was wobbly.

"Yes, imagine spending all that when I could have just put a throw rug over the scorch mark. Well, you've been warned: I'm madly extravagant. Really not good husband material."

"That," I said, "is *not* necessarily what I look for in you." Which is why I kept him a secret from my family, who looked for nothing else. My father would have seen him as an acceptable suitor for a damaged daughter, and my mother would have seen him as a sperm donor.

"Yes, well, we can talk about that later... I didn't take the late flight so we could discuss interior decoration."

And for a while the conversation was mostly nonverbal; our bodies were capable of carrying on a fine dialogue all on their own. After all this time apart, my body's part of the conversation was basically *yes! now! yes!*

"The only thing I like better than you putting on black lingerie for me," he said into my left breast, "is you taking it off for me."

A suggestion with which I was more than happy to comply.

There was a long, slow, tender time that involved a lot more kissing and slow, sensuous movements bringing me to a glow that seemed to last forever. When I sighed, he shivered and said, "*Thalia*," and pulsed deep inside me.

Afterwards he just held me close for a long time, gently kissing my face and neck and breasts. I would have purred if I'd been able to. I had no quarrel whatsoever with Lensky's usual slammed-by-a-tornado approach to sex, but this had been something else. Gentle. Sensitive. Sweet.

"I want to have this all the time, Thalia," he said at last.

"Mmm. Any time." I thought I was agreeing with him.

"No, Thalia. Not any time. All the time. You, here in my bed, every night. Waking up to you every morning."

"You mean... move in with you?" I practically lived here already. But the thought of giving up my share in the apartment with Ingrid made me nervous. Burning bridges.

"No, not just move in with me; marry me. I want you every night and every day. I want all your nights and all your days, forever."

He was serious.

I was terrified.

"Brad, I haven't thought about -"

"Thalia, I've already told you that I love you and that I want a future with you. What did you *think* I meant?"

I had been carefully not thinking about it. It had been safer to live in the moment, the more so when so many of the moments were so extraordinarily good.

"I don't know if I can."

"Get married?"

"*Be* married. I never thought of myself as a.... wife."

Lensky sighed, rolled over on his back and put his hands behind his head. "As I recall," he said finally, "we had to dance around like this for a while at the start, before I finally got you into bed. So I guess I'll have to give you some time, again, for your feelings to catch up with mine. Only... Thalia, don't take *too* long?"

I could hear the tension in his voice. Things flashed through my mind at light speed. The terror I'd been feeling, off and on, whenever I realized how important he'd become to me. His face when he thought me dead. The warm security I felt in his arms. Protectiveness that was sometimes annoying. A sense of being loved and accepted that I'd never known before.... "Yes," I said.

"Yes, you'll think about it?"

"Yes, I'll marry you."

Keep reading for a sample from *A Tapestry of Fire*,
the fourth book in the Applied Topology series.

# Wimberley, Sunday

The guest house was actually two buildings: a narrow three-story frame house and a long, low and much more modern building of native stone, which was where the office was located.

Getting to the Inner Light Guest House outside Wimberley this afternoon had supposedly been so urgent that nobody had time to brief me, so urgent that I couldn't take time to look the place up and get an idea of the setup, so urgent that I had to throw a few respectable clothes into a suitcase and take off with faith that the GPS in the car would find the place. But apparently it hadn't been urgent enough for one of the owners to wait in the office and give me a clue where to go next.

I dropped my suitcase on the stone-flagged floor and headed for one of the squashy leather sofas under the chandelier. Doubtless not where the hired help were supposed to hang out, but I could hardly be blamed for that, could I?

I had just sat down when I heard a couple of people laughing and joking outside. The French doors opening on the deck out back were brilliant with afternoon sunlight; the couple who stepped inside paused for a moment, blinking, no doubt readjusting to the shadowy interior. My new bosses? No, they looked too young, too rich and too carefree to be the Fosters. Guests, then; some of the people I would be expected to wait on as soon as the Fosters turned up and briefed me on my duties.

"Oh, you're here already!" the girl, a lanky brunette with an incipient sunburn on her exposed shoulders and midriff, squealed as soon as she registered my presence. "*Isn't* it *marvelous*, Chet, she won't miss any of the activities!"

The young man with her looked like a Chet. Probably short for something like Chester Allandale Whitehead III. Artfully cut blond hair, horn-rimmed glasses, designer shirt, khakis: he could have posed in *GQ* over a caption like, "Weekend Chic."

The brunette closed in on me while I was making these observations. "Hi, I'm Ginny," she said, holding out her hand, "and you must be Sally. I do hope we're going to be friends."

Sally, yes. Potential friend, no. "I think there must be some mistake," I said. "I work here – that is, I hope I'm going to work here. Is Margo Foster around anywhere?"

Ginny dimpled. "Oh, don't bother with that silly cover story!"

Damn. Busted *already*? I was going to have a hell of a time getting out of this big, squashy sofa. And then there would be the problem of running in these high-heeled sandals. I hadn't exactly dressed for flight. But then, hadn't it been reasonable to expect my cover would hold up for more than fifteen seconds?

In emergency, I could always teleport, but we were discouraged from doing that in view of outsiders. Maybe I could sneak out using Camouflage.

"The Fosters told us at lunch that you'd be coming," Chet said.

"But you don't really expect us to believe that you're just some extra help they've hired, do you?" asked Ginny. "Not after that story in *Whirred*?"

What story?

"We know you're here to spy on us," Ginny said. "But it's just silly for you to pretend to be some little waitress, especially after that photograph! We don't have any secrets! We all talked it over after lunch and decided the best thing was to include you in all the retreat activities. After all, the whole point of the retreat is for us all to get to know each other better and make a stronger team. And obviously you're going to be a team member – at least I hope you will."

"What photograph?" This time I said it aloud.

"Just this afternoon. Didn't you see it? I've got my phone set to alert me every time there's a new posting on *Whirred*. They have all the *best* Austin-area industry gossip and usually before anybody else." Ginny's coral-painted nails tapped at the surface of her phone. "See?"

The words "Secret Love" dominated the screen. The man who was the reason for my coming here was pictured just below that, with a paragraph of dreadfully coy, gossipy innuendo about how the reclusive Austin financier Shani Chayyaputra had lost his heart to a certain young lady. Below that was a blurred picture that, okay, could have been me. Could have been almost any short girl with spiky black hair, though.

"Mr. C. probably thought it would be funny to slip you in here without telling us who you really are. Tell the truth now: didn't he want you to find out what we say about him behind his back?"

"He never suggested any such thing to me," I said with perfect truth.

"And is your name really Sally? Or is that just part of the cover?"

"For now," I said, trying to look knowledgeable and mysterious, "Sally will do just fine." And if I was slow in answering to that name, well, they'd already come up with an explanation for that, hadn't they?

"But you *are* Mr. C.'s fiancée," Ginny pushed.

I looked at my nails. "I wasn't supposed to…"

"It's all right," Ginny said, "when he gets back we'll explain to him that you tried to slip in incognito but we saw through your act. He can hardly blame you for the fact that you couldn't fool a group of brilliant, highly intuitive people with a particular talent for seeing hidden connections!"

When she put it that way, I had to admit that it seemed silly even to try.

"And I *love* your belt," Ginny added. "Did Mr. C. give it to you? Is it, like, some piece of antique Indian jewelry?"

I warmed to her. Some people thought that the belt of silver scales, finished off with an elaborate silver knot around a beaky protuberance, was a bit excessive on somebody as short as I was. "Actually," I said, "it's Mesopotamian."

Chet looked down his patrician nose. "I heard a lot of Iraqi national treasures disappeared from their museum during the war."

"Well, this isn't a museum piece," I told him. Even if part of it was three thousand years old, the rest was all modern manufacture. And I hadn't gotten the authentic part of it out of a museum; I found it in a turtle pond. Or you could say that it found me.

I wished one of the Fosters would turn up. I wanted to unpack. I wanted a shower. And most of all, I wanted to get away from ebullient Ginny and patrician Chet, and call the Center for Applied Topology to find out how I was supposed to handle this.

Not that anybody I could ask was likely to have a good answer.

Like an answer to prayer, a slim middle-aged woman in leggings under an embroidered tunic glided into the room. "I'm Margo Foster," she announced. "And you must be Sally. Come along now, you've barely time to change before we start serving dinner, and you certainly can't wait tables in those heels."

"Oh, Sally isn't going to be working here as a waitress," Ginny said.

Margo Foster managed to raise one eyebrow without disturbing her makeup. "She isn't?"

Ginny produced a positive shower of dimples. "She may have fooled you and David, but *I* stay up to date with industry news!"

"Industry gossip, anyway," said Chet.

"Oh, you!" Ginny elbowed him and giggled. "Sally is Mr. C.'s mysterious fiancée. He sent her down here to report on how we talk when he's not around, but *I* saw through her at once!"

"You… did?" Margo couldn't frown; it would have cracked her makeup. The most she could manage was a slightly puzzled expression.

"She had to admit it when I asked her straight out, didn't you, Sally?"

"Oh, well, in that case…" Margo's voice trailed off.

"She needs to join the retreat with us," Ginny said. "That way we'll *really* get to know all about her."

Oh, I hoped *not*.

"And she'll know all about us."

At last, something consistent with my original plan.

"Now don't be difficult, Margo darling," Ginny urged. "You know there's plenty of space. Your brochure says you can handle groups of up to ten, and there are only six of us – well, seven, now that Sally's come."

"And how am I supposed to handle *any* groups without a waitress?" Margo snapped.

Ginny shrugged. "Put out everything buffet-style," she suggested, "and we'll serve ourselves. Nobody will mind. And now that we know who she really is, we'd be *much* more uncomfortable having Sally wait on us!"

By the time I got to the bedroom Margo had hurriedly assigned to me (quite an upgrade, I suspected, over the lodgings for the hired help) I was exhausted just from agreeing with Ginny's assertions and saying nothing that would contradict the story in her head. Well, actually that second bit wasn't too hard; what *would* have been difficult was getting a word in edgewise.

Ginny would probably have been exhausting even if I hadn't been acting a part; that woman should come with a warning sign reading CAUTION – HIGHLY INTERACTIVE. Pretty much the exact opposite of me, that way.

Once alone, I sagged down on the end of my bed and tapped the ornate flourishes of my belt buckle. The tapered silver coils unwrapped; the turtle head looked up at me with bright black eyes. Mr. M. slithered out of my belt loops and undulated across the floor to the bureau. (Mr. M. is short for Mr. Mesopotamia, which is what we called him after it became clear that our American tongues were never going to wrap around a Babylonian name that *started* with 'Niiqarquusu Adrahasis Galammta-uddua' and went on from there.) Anyway, there he was on the floor, giving the bureau the evil eye.

"Climbing this thing will be too much work," he complained. "I need coffee."

"Fly?" I suggested.

"That is even more work. Coffee!"

I was *not* going to deal with a hyper-caffeinated, snake-bodied turtle mage on top of everything else. He would never be able to hold still enough to pass as an ornate belt if he got into the coffee. Worse, he'd probably want to sing.

Instead, I scooped him off the floor and set him on the top of the bureau, where he promptly arranged himself in a spiral around a ceramic candleholder.

"Mr. M., what am I going to do now?" I asked him. "I was going to be a *waitress*. A semi-invisible servant. I can't possibly pass myself off as Shani Chayyaputra's fiancée!"

"The role is, indeed, loathsome and abhorrent," Mr. M. agreed, "but since you are not required to consort with the man in person, I see no reason why you should not allow these people to believe what they will. Participating in their planned activities should give you a far better chance of penetrating SCI's secrets than merely eavesdropping on them at their meals."

"Yeah, until they see through me. Then what?"

"*If* they suspect you," Mr. M. said cheerfully, "then boot, saddle, to horse and away! Or, to be literal, *Brouwer!* and away!"

"If I have to teleport out of this mess," I said, "Chayyaputra will know *exactly* who's been spying on him."

www.ingramcontent.com/pod-product-compliance
Lightning Source LLC
Chambersburg PA
CBHW061207170626
46809CB00003B/1281